A HOUSE IS A BODY

A
HOUSE
IS A
BODY

STORIES

SHRUTI ANNA SWAMY

ALGONQUIN BOOKS OF CHAPEL HILL 2020

Published by
ALGONQUIN BOOKS OF CHAPEL HILL
Post Office Box 2225
Chapel Hill, North Carolina 27515-2225

a division of
WORKMAN PUBLISHING
225 Varick Street
New York, New York 10014

Grateful acknowledgment is made to the editors of the following journals, where these stories first appeared: *Black Warrior Review*, for "Blindness"; the *Kenyon Review Online*, for "The Laughter Artist"; *West Branch* for "Wedding Season"; *AGNI* for "A Simple Composition"; the *Boston Review* for "The Siege"; the *Paris Review* for "A House Is a Body"; *McSweeney's Quarterly Concern* for "Mourners"; *Joyland* for "Didi"; and *Prairie Schooner* for "Night Garden." Additional thanks to Laura Furman for her inclusion of "A Simple Composition" in the *O. Henry Prize Stories 2016*, and "Night Garden" in the 2017 collection.

LIBRARY OF CONGRESS CATALOGING-IN-PUBLICATION DATA

Names: Swamy, Shruti, [date]– author.
Title: A house is a body : stories / Shruti Anna Swamy.
Description: First edition. | Chapel Hill, North Carolina : Algonquin Books of Chapel Hill, 2020. | Summary: "In this collection of stories, dreams collide with reality, modernity collides with antiquity, myth with true identity; women grapple with desire, with ego, with motherhood and mortality. The stories travel from India to America and back again to reveal the small moments of beauty, pain, and power that contain the world"— Provided by publisher.
Identifiers: LCCN 2019059046 | ISBN 9781616209896 (hardcover) | ISBN 9781643750606 (e-book)
Classification: LCC PS3619.W3524 A6 2020 | DDC 813/.6—dc23
LC record available at https://lccn.loc.gov/2019059046

10 9 8 7 6 5 4 3 2 1
First Edition

For Abe.
With love so vast, I can't see to its other shore.

CONTENTS

BLINDNESS

SUDHA AND VINOD had a modest wedding. At their parents' insistence, Vinod had ridden in on a horse. It was wedding season in Delhi, and every night the streets were filled with the raucous dancing of the families of bridegrooms, the weather gentle, still a few weeks away from ferocious heat. Sudha's body was covered in turmeric the night before. She didn't think she would enjoy it, but there was the undeniable pleasure of being touched by so many loving hands. The turmeric was cool, and resembled in texture and consistency the river-mud of her mother's ancestral home, where she had swum summers as a girl. She also took a milk bath. How do you feel, her mother asked her, bathing her like she had when Sudha was a child, and because of this, Sudha had not felt any shame in her nakedness.

Fine, said Sudha. She smelled of bitter herbs, but tomorrow she was promised she would look beautiful. When she got out of the bath her mother rubbed her down vigorously with a rough towel.

And your wedding night?

What about it?

Are you ready?

What is there to be ready for? But then she smiled at her mother and her mother knew that she was just teasing. At night some weeks later Sudha and Vinod climbed up to the roof of their new flat to smoke a cigarette. From somewhere in a twist of road below them they could hear the brass sounds of the wedding band. They didn't speak, just passed the cigarette back and forth. There was a cap of smog that made the sunsets blaze with color but obscured the stars. Sudha took her husband's hand. It was thin and dry and warm. She had memorized the lines in his palm, cut deep as though in wood. She listened to the sound of his breathing. Once she had lain on top of him, very still, and kept her face close to his so that she could taste the air that came from his mouth, tinged with clove from the kernels he sucked for better digestion.

Do you find me handsome?

Do you?

Yes, he said, smiling his kind smile, I find you very handsome.

I do too.

We'll have to stop smoking these things soon. They'll kill us.

Is that what you're thinking about?

No, he said. I was thinking about the time you tried to teach me how to swim and I nearly drowned. Do you remember?

I remember.

How old were you, nine?

I was eight, you were nine.

Did you find me handsome then?

No. I wasn't thinking like that.

The music from the street faded. There were kites in the air, but who was flying them? It was late, and Sudha felt tired, leaning against the concrete railing, her lungs full of the smog of the old city. It felt close to dawn, though it was not nearly that late: the sky was a deep purple. Downstairs she took off her clothes, and lay down naked in the bed. Her body took to water, while Vinod's rejected it, and he had flailed his skinny arms wildly, his mouth gulped down lungfuls of river. At first she laughed, thinking it was a joke; then, with effort, she pulled him out. In her mind as she fell asleep: a cigarette, a river, a baby, and her husband's eyes, the same dark eyes of that drowning boy.

Do you love me? she said.

I love you, he said. He entered her. She had pushed her dress up around her breasts and pulled aside her underwear. She closed her eyes. Look at me, he said, but she couldn't look at him. When Dhritarashtra's mother coupled with his father with her eyes closed, her son was born blind. Look at me, he said again, but she still wouldn't. Fear, a sick-good feeling, tenderness, a strange terror. Hush, she said, and he bucked against her, breathing hard on her. The sound of his breathing was like a train she was trying to catch. She raced after it and she knew that if she could leap onto it, it would carry her away.

Should I stop? he said. Sudha—

Don't stop, she said, and thrust him deeper. He pulled out and came on her belly. They lay beside each other not touching. She didn't move to wipe his semen off her belly. It was warm, the air was warm, the sweat on his back dried against the sheets and thickened into the fabric. Things that seemed like they should be disgusting were suddenly not disgusting. She was amazed by this.

In July a black feeling returned and she left work early, rode the Metro home and sat on the hard divan in front of the television, muted, not really watching anything at all, sitting in the living room and gazing at the actors' lips shaping soundless words. Vinod found her like this and tried to speak to her, but she felt he was very far away. She was all blurry, translucent and unreachable, and she watched Vinod as he paced around the living room in great agitation. What is the matter? he said.

I don't know, she said. She could feel the voice in her throat, but it didn't sound like her own.

Should I call someone?

Call who?

A doctor? Your mother?

She shook her head. I'm fine, she said. When she was a girl she would fall asleep on her arm, and turning in the night she would wake and realize her body had pressed the blood out of it, and heavy, it became a stranger's arm. In the minutes before the needling pain came, she would touch it with her other hand, running a fingertip along the skin of her forearm, the fine hair, the burl of her elbow. It was then the feeling arrived, but on those nights she had felt only the first pricks of it, the way a person crushed to death by stones might enjoy the first on his chest, the pleasant heaviness of them, the way they make the body feel smaller, or held in an embrace.

She did not know how to explain it, so she stayed silent until it passed, and then gorged herself on the cold dinner Vinod had prepared, sat in bed beside him, watching his fingers twitch in sleep.

Three nights later at dinner Sudha wondered what it would be like if Vinod died. The thought came suddenly, and afterward she was surprised she had never considered it before. It was a hard ball bouncing in the pit of her stomach, *he won't* and then *he will* and then *but not for a while* and then *what will I do* and then *I'll have no one*, and his mouth opened, and the pinkness of it inside, the dulled color of blood, but it was empty now, lips forming words, she could see him on the road, dying in a car accident, and she pushed out of her chair and went into the bathroom and screamed against a balled up towel.

He came into the bathroom, and touched her arm. It was smooth tile and concrete in there, and the evening was coming cool now after so much heat. He said her name. It felt nice to hear her name in his mouth, in his voice. She had been putting in long hours at work, which sometimes held the feeling at bay. Architecture was a worship of logic and clean lines; she worked for hours without stopping. Then the weight came. He said her name again. He was fourteen, she was thirteen, they were smoking their first cigarette together on a Bombay beach, far away from parents. He had a girlfriend already, not Sudha, but some other girl, Sudha was in love with Amitabh Bachchan. There were elephants on the beach and it was warm but not hot, the half constructed bridge hung out over the water, a bridge to nowhere. Thirteen was not too young to know you were happy, and it was a comfort to her now, to know for certain, for one moment, she had been. Later in the evening he cried in her arms in the bedroom, and she knew that he had decided to leave her, but she said nothing, just held his face in her hands and let him cry, wiping his tears away with her nightgown. He left three days later, and watching him, the dark of his hair hovering over his white-shirted torso as he had hailed a rickshaw, she felt for a minute that she would not be able to bear it alone. But soon the feeling dulled into tiredness. The heat dried everyone out. At the end of the day you felt you would crumble like old paper. If you cut open your veins, dry blood would pour out like sand.

Late morning, Sudha awoke, pregnant. She felt it suddenly, she knew, despite what the doctors had said. There was a thin film of sweat on her chest. She went down to the train station, fighting against the crowd at the ticket counter. Her body made decisions of its own accord, elbowing itself to the front of the counter and sliding her money, sweat dampened, to the sleepy man on the other side of the glass. Then she went to look for the right platform. The day had not yet reached its apex, still the sun was hot enough to make her perspire, even shaded as she was by the corrugated tin awnings. All around her the porters, with their red uniforms and perfect posture, climbed up and down the long flights of stairs to the platforms with suitcases balanced on their heads, travelers following behind, like children. She wiped her brow with the back of her palm. Her breasts felt sensitive and full.

She found her platform and waited. The train was due soon. A child approached her, barefooted and dressed in a shirt that was once white but now was brown. His eyes were lucid and rimmed with a yellow crust, teeth in his mouth crowded together. He stretched out his hands. Madam, he said, please madam, I'm hungry. Very hungry. He motioned to his mouth. She could sense the presence of a girl, his younger sister, somewhere behind, a girl in a dirty frock and the same bright, yellowy eyes. Please madam, food madam, I'm very hungry. Sudha had left her city eyes behind. She went to the stall where they were selling samosas and bought him five and then thrust them in his hands. And then he was off; the crowd had eaten him. She leaned over the tracks and retched a clear liquid and when the nausea passed she closed her eyes.

Where are you?

I'm on the train.

What train? Are you crazy? Mr. Malhotra is asking for you. The clients are here in fifteen minutes.

I have to go to Rishikesh.

But why? Where are you?

I'm on the train.

Well, get off the train.

I can't now. Tell him it's an emergency. Please?

I can't hear you. The connection is bad.

I said, can you tell him it's an emergency?

Okay. I'll tell him. Are you alright?

Everything's fine, Sudha said. The train clattered against the tracks. Outside the window, the wide green fields filled with afternoon sun, the nameless cities, villages full of children with no mothers. The train drew parallel to an empty riverbank, and the sky was full of birds and kites made tiny with distance. I'll be fine, she said into the phone, and said it again after her colleague had hung up.

She reached Haridwar in the evening. Her bag was small, but still she had to wrestle it from the hands of a porter, who had taken it from her as soon as she had disembarked. It was cooler up here. She felt drawn toward the river, not cluttered with pilgrims as it would be in Haridwar, but soft and empty in the evening light, unworshipped by droning priests and their strict adherents. In Rishikesh, a bend in the river. Birds, animals worshipped there, fish, snakes, ashes. Rishikesh, even the name in her mouth felt cool, like water running against a great thirst. She got a taxi. Haridwar was lighting up in dusk, and the sky got darker as they drove, the lights in Mussoorie like low stars against the black hills. It would be cold in Mussoorie this time of year. The town was made for honeymooners. She had gone there with Vinod before they were married. They had pretended they were in order to get a room. She had been wearing a sari to make herself look more wifely. Vinod brought brandy and they drank it from the bottle; later she had been sick.

When Sudha arrived at the ashram in Rishikesh they showed her to a small clean room with brick walls, and a window that looked out onto the sleeping river. She fell asleep and had a dream. She was a woman with two children. Her husband had died in a roadside accident. She lived now with the children at her husband's brother's house, in a small room beside the kitchen that had been intended for servants. She fed the children as best she could, but at night she remembered only the saddest part of the fairytale to tell them. The mother in that story was so poor that after she finished cooking for her rich sister-in-law, she saved the water she washed her hands with for her children to drink. The little bits of atta on her hands turned the water a milky white and that was all she could offer to her children's hunger. In the story the mother was a good woman and her sister-in-law was a bad woman and god treated them accordingly; punishing the sister-in-law with shame or death, and rewarding the mother with riches—she couldn't remember that now. All she could remember was the bowl of water the mother gave her children, how she watched her children raise the bowl to their lips and drink it, how she forced her lips into a false smile. How at night, the three of them sleeping in the same bed, not a bed but a narrow mat on the floor, breathed heavily in hungry, shallow sleep. She broke off in her telling, watching her children sleep. They needed new clothes. The little one, a girl, was just turning six, with the river colored skin of her father and thick dark hair that her mother had taught her how to comb by herself. Her brother, ten years old, looked like his mother. Someone had given him a pocketwatch. She had taken it away because she thought he would break it, but then he was so angry he wouldn't speak to her for days, and his uncle—her husband's brother—had prevailed upon her to give it back. They were sweet children. They went to school, they came with her in the afternoons to the houses she cleaned and sat quietly and did their school-work and sometimes the good woman she worked for would give them each a glass of milk. She worked for the good woman on some days, but the other women whose houses she cleaned wouldn't even allow her children inside, so she had to send them back to her husband's broth-er's house, pressing down, as she did this, a bad feeling, like shame.

The dream-woman remembered when her son was born. They were poor but her husband was still alive. She held her new baby in her arms and felt love and terror in equal parts. He was tiny—he had been born a few weeks premature. A warm, breathing creature in her arms but it was as if he was made of glass. What if she dropped him or he came by some way to harm?

Do you love me? her husband's brother said.

I love you, she said. He entered her. She had not taken off her sari, she just bunched it up around her waist. She closed her eyes. So many times she had done this now in the small hours of night, night after night, she no longer felt like crying. She hardly felt anything at all. Her mind climbed out of her body and observed the scene from the vantage point of the ceiling fan. With her eyes closed she could see two people moving together, just two dark bodies. Look at me, he said. She wouldn't look at him. When Dhritarashtra's mother submitted to his father with her eyes closed, her son was born blind. I said look at me, he grunted, but still she wouldn't. Hush, she said, and he bucked against her, breathing hard on her.

Want me to stop? he said, mocking.

Don't stop, she said. He pulled out and came on her belly. They lay beside each other not touching. She didn't move to wipe his semen off her belly. It was warm and everything in the room seemed simple and very real: the rattan chair, the clean floor. Things that seemed like they shouldn't be disgusting were suddenly disgusting. She was amazed by this.

Who had given the boy a pocketwatch?

She lay awake some nights. The bodies of her children next to her, smelling of rubbery sweat and soap and scalp. She touched their backs lightly with her palms. They didn't wake. If there was a way to stay like this forever, the three of them sleeping together on the same mat, the children happy in dreams and hunger forgotten, safe, and quiet. If there was a way to keep them forever, never growing old or ungrateful or sour or angry. Each moment became unbearable. If she could weave armor for them from her own skin and hair. She knew the hardness of the world, the meanness. She would carry it forever if she could, carry it alone.

One afternoon she looked at her face in the mirror she was cleaning. Her children were not with her. The bathroom was empty. It was a fancy one with a western toilet; she cleaned that too. Then she turned and there was her face. She looked at it for a long while; she felt as surprised as if she was looking at the face of a stranger. She looked older than she was, with gray starting in at the temples, and her skin folding at the corners of her eyes. She was no longer a girl, but she could see the girl of her face there, in the fullness of her lips, in the darkness of her irises, the soft folds of her eyelids, and that girl's face was pressed over her face like a ghost, the face of her daughter not yet grown or maybe a daughter who was not yet born, or just the face of any young girl, a quiet girl who absorbs everything she sees, everything becomes her, a girl so full of anxious love for the world she is bursting with it. And then another moment passed and her face was her own again, and she was relieved.

The girl was crying when she came home, but the boy was nowhere. Where is your brother? she asked the girl. The girl sniffled and wiped her face. She pointed to the bedroom, the one the uncle and the aunt shared. He said I couldn't come, said the girl, but I get so sad and lonely sitting outside waiting for him. But he won't let me in, he never lets me in.

The mother went to the door and opened it. She knew what she was going to see before she saw it—the uncle startled, the boy mute. She knew it, maybe she knew all along. But she had no other place to go.

Sudha woke up. The light was shining on the river, shining hard through the window. It was still early dawn. She dressed and went to the river. She was in the foothills and they were green. She climbed down the narrow concrete steps of the ghat until she got to the last one that remained above the water. It was always quiet here, an early morning stillness that lasted into dusk. For a while, she stood at the edge of the water. There was no one around. There used to be elephants in the jungle on the other side of the river—she had seen them through binoculars as a child. There weren't any more. The jungle was thinning out, even as the river swelled.

When she looked into the river she saw a face. The face in the water was dark-skinned like hers but had wrinkles around the eyes and mouth. She looked tired and sad, something in the eyes told her, dark but not dull, the small frown in her mouth, and she saw a sigh form on the lips of the face. The face looked like her mother's face or her grandmother's face, and yet she could find hers in it too. There was a moment where the two faces lay perfectly still on top of each other—and then the reflection was just her own again.

She let each feeling rush into her belly and lie there. He was there, knotted inside her and growing, in another month her skin would start to stretch to accommodate him as he grew lungs and fingernails, his little heart beating like a moth. She let dread wash over her, and love, and fear, and anger, she started to laugh though there was no cause, and she thought *I must not be frightened now.* She remembered the baby from her dream, the baby she held in her arms, she remembered her own mother. The feelings were a train, driving hard through the center of her, and when they blew clean through the other side, she felt empty of everything, except for him.

MOURNERS

Y OU HAVEN'T EATEN anything," Reggie says. They
can hear Maya with the baby in the other room;
the baby is crying, then being hushed.

"I'm not hungry," says Mark.

"How now, gentle cuz?" Reggie says. She puts her hand
on his rough cheek. Her face is sardonic as always, but
there is kindness in it. Then Maya comes in with the baby,
whose little cheeks are wet with tears. Seeing her father,
the baby reaches her small hands out to him. Maya is wearing a sleeveless dress. Her eyes, thickly lidded, normally
languid, now are red and tired.

"Will you hold her?" says Maya.

"No," says Mark.

Maya looks at Reggie, who opens her arms.

When she learned Chariya had died, Maya immediately
left her small apartment. It was windy in New York; she
wore a coat and gloves and a scarf and a hat. Daylight
passed. She walked by men and women and looked at them

with just her face exposed. But from this small expanse of skin they could read her perfectly. Her mind was stunned, her body hungry, a hunger that frightened her. She slept in her seat with a hand over her mouth while her body flew west: she was dreaming of being fucked. It was Reggie who came to get her at the airport, looking rough in the unfussy clothes of a farmwife, holding Chariya's baby in a carrier. Standing under the arrivals sign, Maya pressed tears back into her eyes with the heels of her hands.

Maya sits in the bathtub for a long time before she puts on the tap. It was Chariya's room, her sea-room, where she had taken long baths, and where she had given birth. Blue tiles, blue walls, blue towels, and a flat, gray light coming in through the window. With her foot, she nudges open the tap, which floods heat. She looks at her body, wavering under the water. What use is a body? There is no milk in her breasts.

"Maya." Mark's voice. It comes from far away, and she lifts her head above the translucent surface, and closes the tap. Then the house becomes silent. He says again, "Maya."

"What?"

"I—I left something in there."

"What."

"My reading glasses. Do you see them?"

"No." Still she can feel him standing, pressed against the closed door. She says, "I found seven white hairs today."

"Where?"

"At my left temple."

"You're young still."

"Chariya is going gray."

"Was." From far away they can hear Reggie with the baby, cooing, the sound an animal makes. The sound of the baby's laughter. She has been fussy, getting her teeth in. But the last few days she has sensed the change in the house and become quiet.

"Maya."

"No," she says.

Five or six, dusk gathers quietly outside until the room is filled with it. White moths spread their wings against the windows, but from the inside they are just their shapes: black. When the baby cries, Maya takes her and rocks her against her body. Soon the baby is sleeping. Maya and Reggie begin to talk about Chariya. From the other room Mark listens to the fall of their voices. They are tender as they speak about Chariya.

"She'd just cut her hair. Did you see it?"

"No," says Maya.

"Short as a man's. Like a French girl's. It suited her."

"People used to think we were twins. But she was older."

"Couldn't have been by much."

"Five years."

"Five? I don't believe it. I thought Irish twins at least."

Mark thinks of the sisters together. They both stand

at the edge of the lake. Chariya is not yet pregnant. One wades in and the other stays on the shore: one dark, the other darker. Then they are each other's reflection. It is Chariya who floats up, arms and hair spread out, in the green water. She is wearing a blue bathing suit that makes the skin of her inner arms and thighs seem golden. When she wants to, she can look sublime, so happy. From somewhere he can hear Chariya laughing, and his heart leaps up. But then he realizes it is Maya. Maya as she begins to hum a song to the sleeping child, a lullaby that Chariya sang too. A lullaby for his daughter, but he accepts it as his. And sleeps.

The women are in the kitchen in the morning when Mark wakes. Reggie's hair is wet, and Maya sits very quietly at the table, with the baby again in her arms. The baby examines a small apple that Reggie has given her. She doesn't yet have the teeth to bite it. She keeps bringing it to her mouth. "Are you hungry?" says Reggie. She gives him a cup of coffee.

"Yes," he says. Maya has dressed herself in a yellow sweater that was once Chariya's, and a soft blue skirt. Reggie is in jeans.

"You were sleeping so deeply we thought you were dead," says Maya.

Mark sits down at the table, facing Maya. Her bottom teeth are crooked. She has never had braces, like her older sister did.

"Don't look at me like that."

"You've got a real wasp problem," says Reggie. She points to the window.

"I thought I got them all."

"Well, you didn't."

"The cold will get them."

"The cold won't do anything. I'll call someone." Reggie is examining his face. He sees himself sitting barefoot in his shorts in his kitchen with these women, and feels ridiculous.

"No, I'll do it," he says. "I'll do it."

It is a task for later, for dusk. Reggie makes eggs. They sit at the table to eat. The baby has set down the apple and is pulling unhappily at her ear. She wears an austere white jumper, and with her dark cap of hair looks a like a tiny monk. Mark has seen a child's skull once, in a medical museum, with all the adult teeth poised under the milk. The skull he saw was older, a four- or five-year-old child. But Mark sees there the skull of his daughter. Quiet bone, and growing, the teeth expanding, creaking like swollen wood as they push outward, slicing the gums. The double grin that lasts in death, while the eyes and nose and ears fall away, become dark holes. He lifts his eyes to Maya, whose chin rests on the baby's head. As she turns her face to glance out the window, he catches his breath. For a simple, brilliant moment, she is Chariya, the cocoa-brown curve of jaw, her fierce eyes, with their curly lashes. He stays very still and looks at her.

"Stop it," she says, feeling him, facing him, and starts to cry. "Can you please stop it?"

Will it rain? Rain trembles in the clouds, but the clouds never break. Mark is tired, Maya is tired, Reggie is tired, tireless. She is mending a burst seam of a coat, Chariya's. Reggie squinting by the lamplight to thread the needle. Why bother?

But she must bother. She has seen Chariya wear the coat again and again. It is the seam that holds together the chest to the arm, under the left armpit, her waving arm. Chariya stands at the gate and waves, the sweater underneath showing yellow at the opening. Chariya's dark face at the gate as Reggie reverses the car and backs down the drive. And Reggie called, "Careful, you'll tear the whole sleeve off." But Chariya had no time to fix her coat—why else did she cut her hair so short? Chariya had no time to comb her hair. Chariya had no time to read a book she loved. Chariya had no time to go to Paris. Chariya had no time to take a nap.

The house is old and shifts on its haunches, settling. Reggie is not startled by the house's noises, she lives just down the road in an old house of her own, but has slept here since death came. Not slept, but laid unsleeping in the room between her cousin's and the baby's, alert always for the mewling cries of the baby as she, hungry, wakes, and alert for Mark, moaning in his sleep, never words, only snuffles and grunts. She can see in his waking eyes the dazed confusion of a very young child. His cheeks dry and sallow as paper, the same cheeks upon which she had kissed her blessings on his wedding day, and kissed blessings against the soft cheeks of his bride.

Reggie drags the thread through the fabric. She is doing her work by sense not sight, following the fabric's curve by instinct. What a violence mending does, the needle piercing and piercing. It is a good coat, a fine coat, one that held Chariya's body for years, even when the belly was swollen with baby and the button could not reach its hole. Finished, she breaks the thread with her teeth and drapes the coat around her own shoulders.

When evening comes Mark ties a scarf around his mouth and takes the poison out. The sky is beautiful, hanging very low down, thick with cloud, and all the trees darken into large shapes in the yard, the apple and lemon trees and the oak. He follows the channel of wasps to its source. Even in the dim light, he can see the nest resting in the space between the roof and the wall of the house. It seems to radiate light, pale as it is, like a moon. Wasps should be killed at dusk, after they have finished their day's work and they are returning home. But last time he hadn't been ruthless. The smell of the chemical sickened him. The wasps were soundless, drugged on fumes. They were dizzy and frightened and didn't try to sting. He felt sorry for them, and had gone back inside.

Now, he watches the last of the wasps fly in. It is fully

dark, but his eyes have adjusted. His hands are cold. Before the chemicals coat the nest and dry, a few emerge, flying weirdly, almost drunkenly, then dropping. He sprays and sprays. The rest are trapped in that house of theirs. They die quietly. The bitter smell is all around him, though he tries not to breathe it in.

Mark walks away from the nest and takes a mouthful of evening, gulping it. The air is sweet and cool, and the stars are coming out. It is only five-thirty. Inside, they have turned the lights on. The house looks cheerful. He has never stood outside his house, just like this, in the dark, alone, looking in. It feels pleasant and comfortable to be cold outside, peering in like a robber, or a child looking into a neighbor's house. He can see Reggie moving around in the kitchen, but not Maya. He removes the scarf, and the cold air enters his lungs. He can feel it in his chest. For a moment he is awake with it, he has finally woken up. He holds his breath. He is so close to it, to feeling joy, the joy of the body. But it is moving away from him. He cannot reach it. The poison in his hand, the dead are dead. The held breath bursts out of him, and is gone.

The top of a tiny white tooth appears in the baby's lower jaw, like the tip of the moon trying the horizon. It is not centered but set slightly to the right. The baby touches the tooth with her fingers. A familiar taste, almost ugly, taste of red. At first there is the pure surprise of newness, where there is no fear. But fear comes. She was once soft, all of her soft. Now there is some hardness stuck in her, pushing out from her. She can feel voice building up in her lungs like heat, voice building and building until it spurts from her mouth. Her sound is a comfort around her, the yellow-orange glow she builds. The tooth in the mouth, and where has mother gone? Mother and not-mother. Mother came when she called, and lifted. Mother tickled and wept. Mother laughed. And father used to kiss gently but with scratch. Now he doesn't kiss her. She reaches and he turns away. Her voice builds and builds and then a coolness comes in her throat, and she quiets. She bats up her fists and feet and kicks, feeling the limbs working below. There is silence at the center. It is courage, the baby. It is the courage to live in an expanding body, with limbs lifting outward, with teeth pushing up, with hands and mind growing finer, with eyes settling on color, with body unbending from the earth and standing upright, balancing perilously on two legs, and then moving forward, walking, running forward, teeth loosing, filling, knees scraped and healing, voice gaining depth and sureness, hips and breasts accruing, skin darkening, stretching, blood slipping out from the thighs, and death always, always, at the back.

Arms go around, arms lift. When the woman looks at the baby in her arms, the baby looks back at her with her color-shifting eyes, gray now, in the kitchen light. The irises are immense, like cat's eyes, with hardly any white, the mouth impossibly gentle. Reggie doesn't want to bless the baby because what good have her blessings done? She moves ice along the hot gums. It clicks against the nub of tooth. They are calm, the woman and the baby. Their silence is mammalian and warm. The woman can smell the milky skin of the baby, the baby can smell the humble soap and hand salve of the woman. It is she, perhaps, who should seek the blessings from this child, who will come to her when she, Reggie, is old, carrying an armful of fragrant lilacs. Placing the lilacs in a vase, as the old woman moves around the kitchen preparing tea. And the old woman draws strength and pleasure, yes, from the fragrant sight of the flowers, but more from the young woman's strong, happy body, the length and gentleness of her limbs, the shine of her dark face.

That night they all eat at the table, they drink wine. It is not good wine, but it doesn't matter. They begin to tease one another, and tell jokes, jokes to shock one another into laughter. Laughter tastes funny in their mouths, mixed with the bitter taste of the wine, then they warm to it. They tell stories of old lovers. Maya rests her bare feet against the legs of her chair, Mark looks at those feet: he would like to become a dog and lick them, and the fat bones at her ankle. A lover who only wanted to fuck in the bathrooms of moving trains, a lover who called for his mother as he came, a lover aroused by the sound of running water. A lover who always kept on his socks. Chariya: Mark would never say it. Crying after she made love, tears beading the small corners of her eyes. But not sad, she said, wiping her face and laughing. Not sad.

"I slept with a white man who kept asking me to talk to him in Hindi."

"Did you?"

"Well, I don't know Hindi. So I just started saying the names of dishes in Indian restaurants."

"That's bad!" says Reggie. "What did he do?"

"He came."

The baby tires. Maya takes her and changes her and puts her to sleep. She stands tipsy in the dark room looking at the child with night-sharpened eyes. The child is curled, her fists, her feet, pulled tightly into herself, impenetrable in sleep. She looks fierce in her crib, giving the profound illusion of self-sustenance. Asking nothing from the young woman who looks down at her, and yet, the question posed anyway. Will she fly home with sleep knotted in her throat, go to work, and have drinks in bars, never marry, mourn alone? Will she remain in the company of these mourners, as the child grows more and more substantial and lovely, and learns the breadth and depth of her loss? She cannot face this question. She wants to wake in her apartment and shake this dream off herself like a wet dog, take a shower, drink strong coffee, and sit in the bright possibility of morning. But morning will never come to her like that any longer. Each morning she will wake with the metallic stain of absence on her tongue.

In the kitchen Reggie helps Mark put away the dishes. But she is suddenly exhausted, and all at once, the light in the room becomes white at the center and expands.

The hand grasping the plate loosens and the plate shatters against the blue tile. She leans against the counter, until Mark's arms come around her and she slumps into the bulk of him, half-awake, half-dreaming, apologizing through furred lips. She can smell his swallowed tears but does not have the strength to feel pity. There is a bright buzzing in her body, the sound of a train. He lifts her above the shards of the plate, stepping carefully around them with his feet in only socks, calm, murmuring to her as he would to a child, saying she's very tired, she needs to rest. She has not been carried since she was a girl, Mark does it easily. For all her solidity and tallness she is light in his arms as he brings her to bed. He inspects each callused foot for embedded slivers of china, and when he finds none, asks her if she wants some water. No, she says, waving him away. She says sorry. "Sorry for what?" She doesn't answer. Sleep hovers above her eyes with milky thickness. Then she has passed through it, without a dream to soften it.

"Did she drink too much?" Maya standing in the doorway.

"She hardly had anything. She's just tired, I think."

"Should we call a doctor?"

"She's alright. Let her sleep."

They return to the kitchen and pick up the broken plate, Maya collecting the fat shards in a bag, Mark vacuuming the kitchen's corners. When the task is finished they leave the dishes where they are and open another bottle of wine. This bottle is better than the first, the bitterness is interesting to hold on the tongue. Maya's teeth get a bluish tint from the wine, Mark can see it when she smiles.

"I remember the first time I met you. I didn't like you."

He is too tired to take it gamely. "Why not?"

"You seemed too golden. A little arrogant."

"I'd never been hurt before."

"But it's not better this way. You're not better. I wish you hadn't been hurt."

He says simply, "No point in wishing."

"You were kind to her."

She puts her foot on top of his foot under the table, and it's cold, he can feel it through his sock. Then she drops her eyes. Her hand rubbing absently the stem of her empty glass. It is a different man she met, six years ago, dressed smartly in a suit. As he has made no effort to dress these last few days, he has made no effort to guard and compose his face. Unshaven, the rough skin of a man, with freckles and creases. She can see the pores on his cheeks. She looks into his face like a palm reader looks at a hand, and sees the future of the face, shock deepening into bitter anger. She sees love for the child spread thickly across the brow. The possibility of cruelty trembling in the tight corners of the mouth. She leans over the table and kisses the mouth softly. Please do not be cruel. The mouth is raw, as though she kisses a wound. For a second their faces hover apart, their bodies are still, as if considering. Then she climbs to him, kneeling against the table to press her body to his. The arms that take hold of her radiate from a desperate body.

They go to Maya's room, not Mark's, and shut the door. She takes off the sweater that was Chariya's and the skirt and lies down on the bedspread. Mark standing over her, looking tender and hostile: a stranger. Her body feels crazy. Please do not be cruel. Looking at her, and she lets him, but covers her face with the pillow. He pulls her to him and tugs her underwear down, looses the breasts from the bra, dark nipples bunched as they meet the blue air. Then he thrusts the smooth warm length of himself into her, slicked with her wet, and she is gripping her legs around him. He lifts her up to him, their bodies pressed together, no space, finally, between their bodies, but the tiny, infinite absence that stays between them. The space is a question the body asks and finds no answer. Why? and Where? and Chariya?

Maya's eyes are open. She sees his ear, the curve of his head, the closed door. She can feel his anger coming through her like venom. But she will take it, his anger, and add it to her own. And warmth collecting at the center of her. She closes her eyes. Finds the body's comfort in another body, the sweat that gathers where they touch. She puts a hand against the back of his head, buries her fingers in the springy hair. Can he feel it, this warmth at the center, gentling? He becomes calm, even as his body reaches the frenzy. The feeling is almost holy. Her hair, loose, the smell of honey coming all around him, falling over his shoulders. Her voice biting at his neck, building, building, then quieting. Joy from the body stumbles outward. They are stunned, scared by this joy. Yet each grasps it, holding it like a wild cat in the arms until it frees itself and bolts.

He puts her down on the bed. She, panting, looks at him. He is more humble than she has ever seen him.

"You want a cigarette?"

"I didn't know you smoked."

"Chariya made me quit. We'll have to go outside."

Maya pauses at the baby's door to check her sleeping. Her mouth is open, sucking. Mark and Maya put on scarves and hats and coats and step through the sliding door to the back porch. He draws a pack of cigarettes from his coat pocket and lights it cleanly. She sticks an unlit stick into her mouth and pretends to smoke. Still drunk.

"Can you feel her here?"

"Can you?"

She shakes her head. The cold burns at their fingertips. They're quiet for a while.

"There it is," he says, and points to the nest. Still bunched in the folds of the house like a tumor. "Will you come back?"

"Don't ask me that yet."

"Oh, have it," he says, flicking flame from the lighter and holding it out. She cups her hand around it. Draws the nicotine deep into her, the tar. There is no moon out, but stars. She smoked cigarettes with Chariya. Home from college for Thanksgiving, and Chariya already working. Snuck booze and cigarettes into their parents' pristine house and giggled like wicked children. An animal noise

pierces the dark: the baby. It is Mark who tamps down the
end of his cigarette and goes inside. Without switching on
the light, he lifts her. It is a strange heft in his arms, his
arms that have missed this weight. Chariya used to scold
him, saying the baby would never learn to walk if he carried her everywhere.

"What is it, honey?"

The baby quiets, becomes watchful. She can smell his
cigarettes, but forgives him.

"She has a new tooth," says Maya, unwinding the scarf
from her throat.

"How about that," he says to the child, rocking her, as
the alcohol leaves his body. Soon she is asleep. The house is
soaked in night: night has contracted like a fist around the
house. No matter. They can light every lamp in the house
until morning burns.

MY BROTHER
AT THE STATION

O N THE FRONT porch, my little brother was sitting
with the neighborhood cat. He was gazing very
intently at it. He had crouched down, meeting it
almost at eye level. At first the cat hissed and raised its skin
like it was scared. Then it settled down and became very
still. It stood with all four paws gathered very neatly and
gazed at my brother with its bright yellow eyes.

"What are you doing?" I crossed my arms. Who ever
wants to be a big sister?

"Nothing," he said. He didn't look up at me. Four years
old and he had just begun to lose his baby fat, but his
hands and elbows were still soft as cheese. His hair was
growing back in from the hair-cutting ceremony my parents had done for him, belatedly, a month or so before. He
had a serious look.

"That's my cat," I said.

"No it's not. It's the Epsteins's."

"That's *my* cat," I said again. It was no use. I used to

catch the cat between my knees and put my nose right up against its dusty belly, pulling in the warm, hayish smell of it. But now their gaze was so thick it was almost physical, a cord tied between them.

"He doesn't like it when you hold him so tight," said my brother.

"How would you know?"

"He told me."

"You're such a liar."

"I'm not a liar," he said.

"Prove it," I said.

"You prove it."

"Tell him to do something."

My brother paused, frowned. "He doesn't want to."

"Yeah, right. I knew you were a liar."

He turned his attention back to the cat. There was a very determined expression on his face. They were quiet for a little while. "Okay."

"Make him jump up to my hand." I stretched my arm out at shoulder level. The cat looked at me, my brother, back at me. Then he leapt at my hand, butted its forehead against my fingertips. For a second I was so stunned I thought almost that I would cry. But I didn't want my little brother to see me cry so I didn't. I gathered myself into a black knot. "Does he love me more than you?"

My brother shrugged.

"Ask him," I said.

"Can't tell you," he said.

"Why not?"

"Ishi says so."

"Who's Ishi?"

He didn't say anything. He didn't even have a mean look on his face. His eyes were so dark it was impossible to tell the pupil from the iris. Three weeks ago when our grandma died he said he could see her standing behind me. But I thought he was just lying or imagining like babies do.

"Ishi says there's a bad black thing in you that eats up the good part."

"Who's Ishi?" I said. "Who's Ishi?"

That night I woke to my father shaking my shoulder in the dark room. "Baby, we have to go," he said.

"Go where?"

Light came in from the living room, and as my eyes adjusted I saw he was dressed. Outside, a row of evergreens that lined the fence between our house and the neighbors' striped the grass with thick shadows. I could see the deck chairs and my brother's tricycle sitting lonely in the yard.

"We have to go to the hospital," he said. "We'll be back soon."

"What's happening?"

"Don't be scared," he said. "Everything's fine."

I got out of bed and followed my dad to the living room. My mother was holding my brother in her arms, sleeping, it seemed, but not quite, for his eyes were glazed and open. There was a strange sucking noise coming from my brother's mouth. His feet were in socks but not shoes, hanging loosely from his ankles. "Go back to bed," said my mother.

"Can I come with you?"

"No, baby," said my dad. He was putting on his jacket. "If we're not back in the morning then Mrs. Epstein will come over. Okay?" And, "Do you have the insurance information?" he asked my mother.

My mother said yes.

I climbed up onto the kitchen counter and watched them leave through the window. After they left I turned on every light in the house. I tried to be excited to be left alone. I switched on the TV. But there was nothing for kids on that late. And my mom didn't keep any junk food in the house. There was nothing bad I could think of doing. My parents already let me jump on my bed.

The house seemed, all at once, terrifically empty. I could hear the moan of a dog coming from outside, or maybe a wolf, though I knew that was stupid. I could see myself reflected in the window, a little girl in a lonely bed, and beyond that the trees turned into the fingers of a monstrous thing. Were my mom and dad coming back? I went outside and called for the cat, and after a while he came. The cat was tight in my arms and even though he squirmed I didn't let him go.

Slowly I started to become aware of the dead, gathered in the corners of the house. I couldn't see them, but I sensed them the way you know someone is standing behind you before you turn around to look. If it was my brother, he would see them, but they would glow for him, beautiful and benevolent as moons. For me, they were leeched of color, their bone-white faces and hands and mouths smelling of rotted wood and leaves. In my mind I could see them circling my bed, their hands reaching, reaching. They were saying—what? Their mouths didn't work. They were trying to tell me something, only I couldn't hear it. What did my brother mean about the bad part eating the good part? Under the blankets I put my head close to the cat's, to feel its breath in my ear.

When I woke up the cat had peed on the rug and my mom was making pancakes. My dad was drinking chai in the kitchen. "How could he have known that?" my dad was saying.

"I don't know," said my mother. She was stirring the batter very hard, which made me think she was angry.

"To hear him say it—I'd never told anyone—and my mother, you know, I wasn't there when she died . . ."

My mother put down the bowl and began to cry. "What are we going to do?"

"We don't have to do anything." He put a hand on her shoulder. "It's okay."

"I feel so crazy—" She saw me, standing in the doorway, and wiped her face. "Good morning," she said.

"Good morning," I said.

"Is that the neighbor's cat in there?" said my mother.
I nodded.

"Go put it out," she said, but didn't scold me. When I

came back she had put a plate on the table for me. She had made a pancake in the shape of Mickey Mouse.

"Is he okay?" I asked.

"He's fine. Sleeping."

I sat down and began to eat. I was very hungry. "Do you want another one?" said my mother.

"Yes," I said.

"This one isn't shaped like Mickey."

"That's okay."

I finished my food and went to my brother's room. He was sleeping on his side with his hands curled into tight fists. He slept with his eyes partially open so you never knew. But his breathing was slow and deep and sometimes his mouth twitched. So still and smiling like this I could pretend that he loved me. I put my face close to his face and put my mouth next to his mouth, so I could breathe his breath. His mouth was sour and spiky, held the ugly taste of medicine. I was so angry. I was strong enough to pick him up and crush him. I really could have. He looked smug. He could have kept them away from me forever if he wanted to. He let out a little mewling noise like a kitten. I spat at him. A globe of spit quivered on his cheek, but he didn't wake.

These days when I sleep on my side, I have to put a pillow underneath my belly to hold it up. I had trouble sleeping even before I was pregnant, unlike my husband, who could sleep through an earthquake if I wasn't there to wake him, which once he did. At university when I slept by myself, night was sticky and unbearable. But now, a body beside me, the night becomes something I can tolerate. I get up and go to the kitchen, and let myself eat something, anything I want. Lately what I have been craving is buttermilk, cool and thick from the fridge. Other times I will drink some hot milk with a little honey in it. I often wonder what kind of mother I will be. My mother used to pray a lot when she was pregnant with my brother. But I cannot whisper like her with the beads. I feel sorry for that.

Five weeks ago I shaved my head. I did it because I got infected with lice from the kids at the elementary school where I work part time, and it was becoming too much of a hassle. I wasn't sure if my head would be lumpy or smooth; my parents never did the hair cutting ceremony for me, only for my brother. I remember how he never even flinched when the priest took out the razor. My husband fit his palm around the base of my skull.

"Your eyes look huge."

"Maybe I should shave my eyebrows for emphasis."

"Don't shave your eyebrows."

"Do I look like a freak?"

He thought for a moment. We were in our kitchen, me on a high stool and he beside me, standing, his hand on my head. "Not like a freak," he said. "But strange. You know, the most beautiful faces are strange. Slightly off-kilter."

"Oh, good. Off-kilter was what I was going for."

"No, I'm not saying it right," he said. He rubbed his hand over my scalp, scratchy one way, smooth the other. Air rested on the crown of my head in a new way, and I felt shivery and light. "You look—beautiful, of course you do. Sort of witchy. Go see for yourself."

I turned to see myself reflected in the dark window. Like a nacreous ghost on the other side of the glass, my reflection gazed back. She looked older, suddenly, than I remembered. Her eyes were big and bruisey, her neck exposed, her ears naked. Was this the face of a bad woman? On the other side of the glass, a cat walked across the top of the fence, one delicate paw in front of the other. I put my hands on either side of my face and stretched my mouth into a grin.

The next day I saw my brother at the train station, which I normally walk by on the way to the grocery store. I was going for milk. At first I wasn't sure that it was him, for I had been thinking about him, and felt for a few moments like my thought had put a wish onto a stranger, and lent him temporarily my brother's face. But not so: it was my brother. Though I had not seen him in many years—indeed, in the space of the many years since I'd seen him, he'd grown from teenager to man—his features had traveled with him to the present, the proud nose and lips that were my mother's, and his strange far-seeing eyes. He looked rough. He had an uneven beard and his fingernails were long, his pants, jeans, were threadbare and his camouflage jacket several sizes too large; still he looked better than I had expected. Actually I had not expected much. Some days I had expected him dead.

I stood on the platform and watched him. He sat on a bench with an intense stillness until the train came. He did not seem to be aware of my presence. Would he look to another eye like a college student, or someone without a home? When the train came I abandoned my milk on the platform and boarded it. I got on the same car through the rear door, and sat a few seats behind him so that I could see the top of his head. The train passed through the unwanted parts of towns, the backs of auto shops, the edges of mall parking lots, the dump, the impassive facades of apartment buildings that housed the poor. Even seated, my back hurt, my feet hurt, my hips were loose and tired. If I had not gotten on the train, I would have been back home by now, drinking milk while I lay in bed and read a book. As though sensing my agitation, the baby began to move inside me, a kind of turning that I found both reassuring and not very pleasant: it was the same feeling you had when a roller coaster tipped into its first descent, or an elevator began to drop very suddenly. At that time in my pregnancy, we wore each other like a kind of weather, the child and me, my moods, I imagined, passing over her like wind or rain, and her movements wild inside me some early mornings like an electrical storm.

If I called my parents now, they would urge me to speak

to him, they would forget what they had promised each other and beg me to offer him money, however much I had, beg him to return home. So I switched off my phone. When we pulled into the final station I followed him off the train and onto the street, simply for the pleasure of watching him walk. The way he moved contrasted with the way I did at any time but especially now, when pregnancy inflected my every movement, making me more clumsy and graceless. Even when my brother was a boy he never slouched, he walked with an unconscious trust of both his body and the world surrounding it. He never hid his fists in his pockets or the folds of his coat, each hand with the bony elegance of cats. Feet too, but those were in busted sneakers whose soles were starting to separate at the toes. His hair was feathered with grease and long, past his ears; his shoulders looked narrow as a child's in his jacket. We walked up the sidewalk of a wide street, then through the press of Market, then up Eddy, where the facades of the buildings were shamefaced and sad. I was having trouble keeping pace with him, slow as I was, tired and thirsty. It was windy but clear in the city with a low winter light. I imagined we were running a race, like when we were young, and at any moment he would turn back to smile at me—see, I'm winning. Only a few feet behind him it seemed impossible that he could not feel my presence, but he didn't turn to look. Perhaps he didn't recognize me, remember me, think of me anymore. But I was not so sorry for myself that I would allow that thought for long.

We got to a small park, he sat, then I did, choosing a bench not so far away. He brought out a cigarette and lit it. I wanted a cigarette—*that* cigarette, the one he held, to press to my own lips. Would I love my child the way my parents loved him, or the way they loved me? It was equal, they had said, you do not love your right hand more than your left. But even then I knew it to be false. You may love your right hand less than the thrilling evanescence of lightning. Which would my child be, the hand or the lightning? Which would be easier to love—to bear?

My brother stared out at the smoke he was making, or through, to the people who inhabited the dirty street. His face had the keen quality of a person reading a book, which is to say it did not look bored, nor occupied in its own thoughts, rather, it was fully present in the direction it pointed. If I were only a little closer I could have caught the smoke in my lungs. But I did not know how to be around animals or ghosts. I held them too tightly. The trick, I think, is to show some interest, but not too much wanting. But what did you do with all that want?

A girl came, a white girl, charging down the street. She looked young, very angry, as she stopped in front of him, pulling the cigarette from his lips and stubbing it out with her toe. Where have you been, she was demanding of him, in a voice loud enough for me to hear her. She had long, light brown hair that looked well cared for, slightly curly and loose, and her skin too looked well cared for, flushed in the cold. My brother looked up at her, unruffled. I could not hear his reply. She sat down beside him and put a hand against his rough cheek. Are you hungry, she asked him. Yes, I saw him reply. Come on, she said, I'll make you something. I felt sorry for her then. No. I felt only envy.

They, together, rose. We walked together for a while, the girl and my brother arm in arm on one side of the street, me, some paces back, on the other. Then they reached an apartment building, and I could go no farther. I watched them disappear behind the glass doors.

What do the dead really look like? Every month the moon grows bigger and bigger, and yesterday I saw it hanging ripe and hard as an apple in the black. I cannot imagine. Just before my brother and the woman went into that building, he turned. He turned to look at me. He opened the door and turned to me and I think he smiled. Looking at me—or past me? I think of this moment so often. I imagine the life nested luminous inside me, he could have seen that, like he could see the faces of the dead. He could have seen a bald woman with red eyes. A stranger, or a sister, or nothing at all. *What do you see?* I should have asked him. Demanded it: *What is it you see, that I cannot?*

THE SIEGE

IT WAS THE priest who smothered the horse. The horse's limbs were tied with ropes strong enough to withstand his panic, as the priest took the horse's head in his arms. Almost tenderly. The body became wilder and wilder and tried to buck itself loose. When he was dead, stallion, black-colored, neck-sweat, they lay the body down and I lay down beside it as I was instructed. I had seen other queens perform the horse ceremony, now I was a queen myself. I was newly married, and young. They daubed my forehead with sandalwood, my forehead, the horse's forehead. I lay facing the face of the horse and I looked into his open eyes.

For weeks, for years, they had been preparing me for this moment, the men, the priests, conferring upon me the shlokas I would recite, mentally or aloud, through the full course of night. The women had prepared me too, told me a truth known only to them: that I would dream a dream that the gods had chosen for me, that the dream, if I heeded it, would prove me. Old queens told me old dreams, the dream that reversed a drought, brought sons—triplets, cured a sick king. Yet, when the mantras began to slow from my lips and sleep took me, I saw behind my eyes nothing like the dreams that others had described. I saw no magic cows, or wizened sages, or women springing from the earth. I saw my city burning. When I woke it was still deep night. The horse's open eyes had a gleam and I could smell him, his dry, dusty smell starting to sour. I touched him. His body had become cold. I could feel the muscles in his neck. I was not supposed to touch him, only to say my mantras. But I had forgotten even though I had practiced for weeks and lay there with my hand on the creature. It was as if this night would never end. I began to whisper to the horse, touching him, his silky ears. We had both been bred and groomed for this night. He had fulfilled his duty as I had failed mine. Dew had gathered in the field and soaked me, I began to shiver. And slowly, slowly, dawn came, the most beautiful I had seen. I bore three sons who lived, and two who died, and a small fish that slipped out too early and who I knew to be a girl. Then I was not young anymore, and took pleasure in my garden.

When I went to see the woman in my garden she was wearing a cotton sari that had once been yellow, but was torn and dirty as a beggar's as she sat under the tree. Her face too was dirty, yet unharmed by my husband's hands. It was slender and symmetrical, her face, but there was something keen there, sharp-eyed as a bird and not quite pretty.

She was frightened when she saw me and began to whimper, but I lay a hand on her cheek, and she calmed at my touch, and began to cry. I asked her if she was hungry, and she shook her head. Her breath was dry and horrible, her body smelled of squat human smells: sweat, urine, shit. I bade my servants bring a plate of nuts and fruit, and a clay pot of fresh water. It was hot, on this day, a fat ominous heat, and I was sweating in my silks. She too was sweating, across her forehead and her upper lip. I had wanted to spend the day outspread in pleasure, a hand dipped into cool water. But the sight of her gave me serious fright. There would be no pleasure, I knew, while the woman remained here.

My attendant poured a stream of water into my cupped palms. I drank. The clay gave it a sweet taste, like the river water of my childhood, in which I swam freely, like a kitchen boy. I could see her watching me drink with resolve to refuse it. But I could see the desire for water plainly. Again my servant poured, and again I drank, lustily, wetting my lips. The third time, I held my hands out to her. She, after a moment of hesitation, ducked her face between my palms and sucked the liquid, wiped her face, and spat, and then held out her hands hungrily, and drank, and drank and drank. When she was sated I washed her face and peeled and fed her pieces of a bright, sweet mango, which I ate from too. She had stopped crying. I asked her if she wanted to bathe and she said yes, so I had my servants bring her a tub of water. When she emerged from it she wore the clean cotton clothes I had brought her, and smelled only of flowers, rose. She was smiling with relief to be free of her animal stink. Luminously beautiful, as youth is, brought back to herself: for an instant I wondered if I had made a mistake. But I put that thought aside. Guests necessitated kindness, this guest above all. When it was time to leave she asked me to stay, and her eyes began to fill again with tears. Like a child I took her in my arms, and told her that she would not be harmed, that she could have anything she desired, food, or drink, clothes, or jewels, or servants. What did she want? To go home, she told me. She only wanted to go home. Then she steadied herself, wiped her hot face with the tail of her sari, and pulled herself away.

In bed that night I asked my husband plainly to let the woman go. At first he seemed irritated that I had brought the subject up, but he willed himself into patience and listened to my misgivings. He was still my old friend. There was a border dispute, he explained. The woman's husband, this king-in-exile, was mobilizing an uprising in the outer territories. Rebellions had to be quashed ruthlessly, as ruthlessly as these men had handled his sister, ruler of the dark woods.

What would an evil act like this do but stoke the fire of these rebellions?

Evil? Who was it that cut off the nose of his sister?

Yes, I had seen that horror. And wept with pity at the

sight of her ruined face, this woman who had danced in my
wedding procession with an untrammeled joy. And yet—
does an evil act beget another? On and on and on and on?
Surely he is the more honorable, just and reasonable and
unruled by emotion.

He lost his patience and exclaimed that a woman
couldn't possibly understand the situation's complicated
politics. This stung, and I told him so; he had never resorted
to this tactic in any of our arguments. He regained himself, his cool, he didn't apologize to me, but his tone was
apologetic, he praised my wisdom in many matters—in
all matters—and nuzzled me, rasp of beard against a bare
shoulder, and said, My heart, let us talk of other things
now. Or better yet, not talk of anything at all.

On the edge of sleep I mused. I was not my husband's
only wife, but long ago I had made peace with my jeal-
ousy: my unease had another source. Something inside him
trembled before her. Her beauty? I had seen more beautiful
within the walls of our palace. Perhaps it was simple pride.
I knew his mind so well I could often guess his thoughts
before he voiced them. But this—I didn't understand. It was
the action of a weak man, one desperate, to take another
man's wife. I fell asleep, and had a nightmare, awoke alone,
morning already, and bathed, and did my morning puja at
the temple. Then I went to see my youngest son. The elder
two were their father's sons, mine was this boy: thirteen,
and gawky, and sweet, and growing, dark-skinned, like his
father, but with my features, the proud nose, the big lips,

the large eyes. He was too old now to let me pick him up
in my arms and cuddle him, but he let me smooth his hair
away from his face, and broke his fast with me after his
lessons were finished from the food on my plate. When he
was little, and asked me how he was born, I told him he was
once a small rabbit, and I carried him around in a fold of
my sari. Before a rabbit? A mouse. Before a mouse? A little
moth that used to perch on my shoulder. Before a moth? A
whisper. He was a plump-cheeked child, shy around men,
his brothers, even his father, but lively around me. Question
after question: What was the shape of the world? An egg.
What was outside the egg? Pure nothing. Why was he a
prince while this teacher a teacher, the sweeper a sweeper,
the nursemaid a nursemaid? We progress this way, I told
him, through many lives, passing from one thing to the
next, burning away our bad deeds, accruing merit, ascend-
ing to the highest plane though effort and discipline. Like
your father. Once he climbed to the top of the world, where
there were two lakes, one freshwater and one salt, and sat
between them for centuries to pray. It was blue, blue, blue
there, sky and mountain and waters, unearthly still, as time
gathered around his body but didn't dare touch. Now your
father is powerful. Like one day you will be. What if I'm
not? What if the gods made a mistake? The gods are too
powerful to make errors. More powerful than my father?

No.

I left him with his archery teacher. I watched them stride
out to the range together, carrying their bows, until they

became small figures moving across the wide green plain. He might have glanced back at me with an expression of anxiety—he was not a warrior, my youngest, though he tried—he was too gentle, and was beginning to feel shame for it.

I took my afternoon meal with the women. My husband's two young wives were shy with me: one pregnant, the other had given birth some weeks before to a girl, who was born too early and stood for some time in the gateway between life and death. The mother was worried and ashamed. I told her that it was a joy to have a girl in the palace after so many bellicose little boys (second wife, her sons would never be kings, we all knew). We went to see the child together after our meal. In the nursery, a big demon woman held the child in her arms, feeding her from her own breast, and stroking the little head with her dark hands. I took the girl in my arms and kissed her, blessed her. She had the smell of milk, her mouth was so tiny and tender, and her eyes were closed.

When I was a girl, I didn't know I was a princess. I thought perhaps I was a boy. I learned astronomy and the plant sciences and read the scriptures, and ran wild when my lessons were finished. I never knew my mother. She had coupled with a god and been turned into a frog by his jealous consort—so my nursemaid told me. My father said nothing about her. Like a frog, I was easy in water and on land, and had the certain coolness of skin that amphibians have. Was I happy? It blurs. I've lived so many years now that I only remember color: yellow, yellow, gold, the royal color, and the jewel tones of the palace garden. One day someone slapped me and reminded me I was a girl, a woman—I don't know who dared, it must have been my father. I bled and bore sons, yes, I was a woman. The girl in my arms would grow, learn words, lengthen, be left one day on the steps of another's palace, a beautiful present, and then we would be instructed to think no more about her. She unwound herself into a cry: live, tiny, sputtering. I gave her back to her nurse.

For some days there was a weight to the air that sat in my ears. Then a storm came; I could see the laundry women running to pull the clothes off the lines. It was warm-rained and gentle, and did nothing but wet the parched earth. My husband did not come for some days to visit me in my chambers. And when he did come, his eyes were febrile and unsettled, and he paced the room a hundred times, walking miles and miles in that room while he talked to me almost unceasingly. It was talk of the girl's stubbornness, that the proud bitch would not yield to either threats of violence or love, that her husband was assembling an army full of undisciplined children, how he had foxed him, this husband, who wandered the earth in search of his lost wife, how he would break her, the proud bitch—

Don't speak like this.

—the proud bitch, how she would one day meet her husband at the Capitol's gates and tell him to find another wife because her heart belonged to another. How it would break him. How it would crush the rebellion before it even began.

Sit.

He wouldn't. We argued. He slapped me for the first time, hard across the mouth. Then he became quiet and we could hear the sea thrashing on the shore. My mouth was warm and wet, I touched my hand to it and pulled away red. He had slapped me because he wouldn't let himself touch her, I knew, and I knew also that he had forgotten himself, he had forgotten everything, for an instant, but his own frustration. He said my name, quietly, but I was afraid to look at him. After a little while he left the room.

The girl gave me some comfort. She ate her food now, took water, but still refused the jewels my husband sent. She had set up her small mat under the ashoka tree and spent the brutal heat of afternoon dozing under its shade. Some evenings I brought her ripe yellow breadfruit to eat, it seemed to delight her, this fruit, and I asked her questions about her exile. She said that she was happiest outside, eating berries, wearing simple clothes, free from the constraints of courtly life. Her husband was teaching her how to swim, how to use a bow. The two men, her husband and his brother, became playful away from the eyes of the kingdom, sparring and joking like teenagers. From her royal life, she missed not her servants, her father, her silk bed—nothing. She had never been so happy.

Color had come back to her voice, and with it, her bearing: she now did not let me see her fear. Her fear she kept for herself in the long waking hours between night and morning when every sound she heard was that demon my husband, come to take what he felt was rightfully his. She hardly slept, her attendant told me, each night, she sang and talked to herself quietly for hours, until her voice was spent. Even then she would sit mumbling to herself some calming nonsense. Her mother tongue.

If she had been a man, she told me, she would have been a hunter.

I would have been a scholar, I told her.

Why not a king?

Being a king means you cannot be anything else: not a lover, not a father, not a son. You forget.

Not my husband.

I smiled. Misery clustered around this unfortunate girl. I could not see what was coming for her, but I could see that. Very well, not your husband, I told her.

It was hot, too hot, for weeks, the crops were beginning to brown and curl. Instead of rainclouds, the sky shimmered with thick flocks of crows. Another horse sacrifice was performed with a younger queen, we sweated, all, through the fire-rites, eyes stung by that holy smoke. And in her dream she sewed a shroud for our husband out of the silk of her own hair.

My youngest died first. I was told he fought bravely. Honor or not, he died, fighting in the garden that sheltered the stolen girl, died fighting not an army but a single creature, the Emissary, who felled him at last with a single, crushing blow. How the Emissary managed to infiltrate the garden was still unknown, he had been sent to deliver the warning of war, and killed my child, and several of our men, fighting with a scary genius, before my elder son bent his knees to the earth and bound his wrists. When they brought the news to me I was in the temple, performing my evening prayers, I was kneeling on the cold marble floor. I thought for a moment quite simply: I will die. I could feel my body reach for death of its own accord. Who sends a little boy to battle? I sat so still I could hear my pulse begin to slow, then to stop. I felt my lungs shut, my blood cool. I died for a long time. But I opened my eyes and found that I was still living.

It was night. I went to see the girl. The garden was in ruins, so they had moved her to a proper cell. She had folded herself up neatly by the window, and covered in moonlight she looked as still and cold as a temple carving. But I came closer to her and saw she was trembling. She had seen my son die. When she saw me she was afraid of me and tried to shield herself with her arms. In fact, she became nearly hysterical. I approached her like I would a deer, walking slowly toward her, talking in a voice that was little louder than a whisper, until I was close enough to her that I could touch her hair. She started at my touch and then calmed, and I stroked her hair. I asked her if he looked frightened. My son, did he look frightened? I could see her considering a lie, and then she said, yes. She said I thought you were going to kill me. She was too thin, this girl. I took her fragile hand. The veins stood out from the flesh like embroidery. She put her arms around my neck and wept into my shoulder, and I stood still, bearing her up. Hush now, little one. I felt her fingers in my hair.

I stayed for several days in my room, looking out at the sea. On the other side of the sea, the Emissary told us, an army was gathering. The shore was so distant the eyes could not reach it. But the army would, and claim all that was ours. That was theirs, the Emissary had said, but I knew they wouldn't stop at the girl.

I thought of all the moments of my son, all the moments he had ever had. I held my mind to them like a hand thrust into a fire. I walked from the window to the bed to the window, again and again, not quickly like my husband, but slowly, thinking of my dead son's curiosity, and of his fear. I had thought that grief would make me brave against the rest of my fears: if the worst had come, there was nothing left to dread. But I was still afraid. I could smell smoke, though my window showed me nothing but the shore and the moonlit water. I watched the sun rise yellow through an eerie haze, my maid told me the fire had already been extinguished but it had done some damage. The air smelled of flesh, and singed hair.

When my husband came to me, five days after our son had died, he was dressed in the white robes of a mourner. I would not speak to him and turned my face away. I was trembling from the force of my suppressed tears, finally they came anyway, leaking out of my eyes. I didn't want to be his soft little woman. He said my name. In his voice was a pure sorrow I had never heard, so perfectly it mirrored my own. I looked at him. His face, ageless for centuries, was older than I had ever seen. He said it was too late. Even if he returned the girl, it was too late.

I told him we still had two other sons.

He said that these sons would avenge the death of their brother. Or, I, he said, and rage came into his voice. He slapped his chest hard with his hands. He said he'd kill the creature himself.

Why did you send him? He was just a boy.

He had wanted to give the boy a chance at glory, conquering an easy foe. It was not battle, and he was not too young, my husband had fought and vanquished at a younger age than him.

He wasn't like you.

He was my son as much as yours.

Why, why? Lust? All this for a fuck?

He said no. He said he didn't owe me any explanation.

I thought of a time when my husband and I had raced across a field of grass. I ran as fast as I could, and he ran just a few paces ahead of me, looking back at me, goading me onward, laughing. We were much younger then. I had felt as though it was I running ahead of myself in my husband. I felt I was running ahead of and looking back at myself and I was also the one behind looking ahead at my husband. We stopped running and gazed at each other without speaking. We were looking at ourselves inside the other person, feeling the resonant core that had hunted its mate through the various births and rebirths. The part that said, yes, you. It felt not like luck but birthright to have found my husband. The way you might enter the house where you spent your early childhood but had never returned since. The memory of the room had the same weight and blur of a dream, yet it existed outside of your mind. Your hand pressed against the cool walls of that house.

We were on opposite sides of the room, and stood and looked at each other. My husband was huge, and handsome, and his face was dark. I felt shocked into my own body and mind; I could not enter his. I could not reach him and was not sure I wanted to. Would he return to me? He had been a good king once, and, even more improbably, a good husband. But he was neither now.

In the weeks that followed, life was oddly calm. I had neither the interest nor the permission to participate in the strategizing, the gathering of troops, the fortification of the Capitol walls. Instead, I worked in my ruined garden. A week was spent clearing the debris. Trees centuries old had been uprooted, I had them hauled away. In a time of peace this wood, prized above all, would be carved into fragrant couches and beds; now the trunks were chopped and burned like cheap firewood. When it was finished the earth was pitted with holes. The rich, loamy soil showed through the torn skin of grass, moist and black. It had a sweet smell. I gathered a handful of it and squeezed it between my fingers. When the army comes, I thought, they will find me here. I will stand here and hold the earth of my son in my hands. I was frightened. I kept squeezing the handful of dirt. It got into my nails. I wanted just to stand there, and I stood for a long while, very still.

The next day I planted new shoots and seeds. I called for the girl and she came willingly. She seemed relieved to be outside. We knelt against the earth together. I told her that her husband was coming for her. She said she knew. A few weeks more, I told her. She nodded. Her arms were stippled with red, where mosquitoes had bitten her. She said that she spent most of the day asleep, or looking out the window. But her dreams were often that she was asleep, or looking out her window, so she never knew when she had been dreaming, and when she had been awake. It got very dark in her cell on moonless nights, and she would open her eyes and think she had gone blind: it was a kind of darkness that didn't ebb as the eyes adjusted. Then she looked at me and said that I seemed frightened. Sad, I told her, with sharpness, but she insisted, frightened. Her husband was good and just and merciful and would spare me when he came. The just and merciful one who watched his brother slice the nose from a woman's face? Then she was angry and looked away.

We began our work. It was a strange sight for the

attendants and guards, two queens doing the work of servants. With a small spade I cut holes in the ground and
placed three or four seeds carefully. Then I covered the
hole I made and gave the earth some water, poured from a
copper vessel. The girl needed no instructions. She seemed
at ease with her fingers in the dirt and her arms covered in
soil. She looked very young and happy, sweating a little as
the sun beat down on her, as it did on me, darkening our
skin. We'll move you back outside, now that everything's
cleared. She nodded. I told her that my husband was a good
man. She didn't say anything. I asked her if she had heard
me. She asked me what I expected her to say. Nothing, I
told her. I wish you knew that he was a good man, that's
all. He had been a good man.

Tell me, do you remember your mother?

She said yes, of course she did.

Not in the abstract, the concept of mother, but right
now, can you remember her?

She said yes.

Tell me what it's like.

She was like hearing your own heartbeat. If you stop
for a minute and are entirely still you can hear it. All along
she's with you, but you never notice until you think to
notice.

Is that what mothers are like, I asked her. Or just her
mother?

Just hers, she thought, though she didn't know. Her
mother was the only one she'd known. Perhaps all mothers
were like that.

I was not with my son in the garden. I wiped my face again.

Maybe not.

When I looked at her there was kindness in her eyes and mouth. It was enough that for a single instant my pain subsided, and, despite everything, joy rushed in to the space it had opened.

My husband continued to visit me at night. He had a manic energy. He seemed almost happy. It was terrible to look at him. I had dreams that they sliced off his head. In my anxiety I would find my sons, smoking with the soldiers, drinking and talking, or strategizing late into the night. Quietly I asked them to surrender themselves to their enemies and be spared what was coming. Of course they balked. Once, the elder got angry and called me a traitor. I could see him lying on the palace floor with flies crawling his cheeks and eyes. And remember the sweetness of his first word—mama—bursting joyfully from his lips. He died first in my dreams, with an arrow in his navel, like his father. His brother died by sword. I held them. I took their hands in my hands and kissed them. I wrapped my arms around their big shoulders and they didn't refuse me, but softened with a mysterious grace and let me. I gathered and kept it, all of it, their voices and their smells and the sound of their rough laughter, and their hands, cut and bruised and strong and tipped with hard yellow nails. My husband told me that if I did not stop my hysterics he would have me confined to my room. I was confined to my room for

several days. I spent most of those days awake but in a
strange state that was neither waking nor sleeping. I was
not hungry and ate only berries, brought to me by the girl.
She looked clean and healthy and well-fed even without
my care. Or maybe it was my mother who put her hand on
my brow. My mother, a frog? She had brilliant, amphib-
ian eyes. I stood in a fire. I could feel my skin burning
clean off, and the pain was a relief. The voices of the dead
reached me, my son, and the not yet dead. I was so afraid
I began to weep. My tears evaporated before they formed.
The fire left only my bones. There was a loud noise like
nothing I have ever heard before, the scream of something
metal. Then, I stepped out of the fire.

It was calm and silent, night. I was alone in my room. I
looked down at my body, lying on the bed, whole, dressed
still in the mourner's white. Dizzy when I sat up. Alone. I
took in a lungful of air. I felt for the place that fear had
been, and couldn't find it. Where was my rage? After some
time an attendant came in and gave me some water to
drink. The fighting had begun, she said. My sons? Gone
to battle. My husband? Leading the charge. She told me
my fever had broken. Had I been dreaming? Yes. Was I
dreaming now?

No, she said. No, I wasn't dreaming.

I bathed and dressed, and went to the garden. The
girl was sleeping lightly under her tree, and woke before I
touched her. Is it time?

Not yet.

She said I didn't look frightened anymore.

No, I said. I wasn't.

She said she felt ashamed.

Why? This has nothing to do with you. We could hear, distantly, shouting, and metal against metal, and a sound like fire. I took her face in my hands. I'll miss you.

She kissed my hands. Small shoots, I noticed, needled the earth, growing imperceptibly from the seeds we'd planted. Even on this night. I plucked one from the soil and put it in my mouth, a bitter green. We sat for a long time together and waited for daybreak.

EARTHLY PLEASURES

I MET KRISHNA AT a party. It's hard to believe that I had even been invited to such a glamorous place. But in those days I had a friend who had a friend who got invited to those things, and once in a while she would ask me to come along. I had one dress I wore each time, and little velvet shoes. I was young, and poor, and often felt a kind of pleasant longing for wealth that I knew would never be fulfilled. I would walk downtown and look with equal hunger at the delicate silks draped over the mannequins in the windows and the finely boned women who wore them on their living flesh, and painted their mouths into red hearts, and their eyes into knives or black holes to put desire into. These women were also at the party where I met Krishna.

In myth, his skin was blue, and in life, his skin was blue too. I had seen pictures of him in celebrity magazines, but he didn't photograph well, and many times held something to cover his face. His skin in those pictures was sometimes a strange blue-black, and other times a paler shade, a sky at five-thirty in summer, when the sun was starting to think about setting. Outdoors he always wore sunglasses so that people could never see his eyes. I had looked at those pictures many times since I was a girl, and bought the magazines just to keep looking at him. There was something ugly about him that compelled me. Ugly—or hurt—or a kind of longing that seemed difficult to articulate. It was not that I felt sorry for him, rather, I could imagine having a conversation with him. I felt he could sense in me something secret; his gaze, screened by the sunglasses, the book or jacket he held up to block his face, still seemed tangible, and called out to me. I felt like I must be imagining this connection, but I didn't want to lie. It was there, to me.

The apartment was so large it was a surprise for it to be in a city; it felt like someone's country mansion. The colors were muted. People glittered in it, talking quietly with drinks in their hands. I, the friend of the friend, and the friend, gave our coats. I didn't feel any shame over my dress, which was black, and had been bought secondhand, so it was a little threadbare—I had replaced a missing button at the waist with a small brass safety pin. I was perversely proud of my dress and my large peasant hands with their unvarnished nails. I took a drink from a tray and looked out the window, where the city glimmered as though it had been purchased for exactly that purpose. Then I turned my eyes all over the room and saw Krishna.

He was not wearing sunglasses. When he lifted his eyes to me for a moment I felt the wind knocked out: I was a bell, and he'd rung me. I've never felt the gaze of another as a physical force. We wondered: was he a god? His brilliant eyes revealed nothing. He was brighter than I expected, blue as a peacock's neck. Wearing a simple suit, white shirt, navy jacket, and no tie. His long dark hair was knotted up at his crown.

Frankly, he was surrounded. The entire party circled him, as if without knowing it. Even the people at the outer edges turned their bodies unconsciously toward him. The friend of the friend whispered to the friend, "I didn't think he'd be here."

"You know him?"

"Sure, we've met a few times. Travels a lot."

"What's he like?" I asked.

The friend of the friend smiled with her beautiful painted mouth. "Char-is-ma-tic."

I could call home and tell my mother: this was my glamorous city life. She had told me stories of him at bedtime, so I had slept and dreamed of him. Tell her they had followed him to the bathroom, gone out to the balcony and offered him their cigarettes, tripped over themselves to get him a drink, and I had watched him downstairs hail a cab, and disappear into it, without being able to say one word. What would I have said? In the morning, I drank a cup of coffee black, and sketched his face on the newspaper. My hand seemed to be moving of its own accord. It was a cold morning with a thick mist that came up from the bay, a gloomy morning that made the city seem built only from ash, fog, and iron. I had a hangover that made my mouth feel dry, and there was a headache building at my temples. I wanted that good cold air on my face.

Outside, the streets were empty—it was too early for brunch. Most people weren't awake yet. I pushed myself down into my coat, ducking the bottom half of my face into my scarf. I felt as though I was looking for something, for someone—yes—for him. I imagined him, alone in his five-star hotel where he could watch the city from a magnificent height without getting out of his bed. It was mysterious what he did, how he spent his time. He didn't claim to be anything. Sometimes he brokered treaties between countries, and taught philosophy classes at universities in Delhi and Paris. It was rumored that he had danced with Baryshnikov in New York one surprise summer season. The day my father died, I saw an article in the newspaper about Krishna's peace talks in the Middle East, which had ended in nothing definitive, but had set a new course for diplomacy. I pictured him in the desert, his eyes shielded against the glare by his movie star glasses. He wouldn't be wearing sunscreen: I knew his skin, like mine, was too dark to burn.

When I returned to my apartment, my skin felt burning hot. I removed all my layers and stood at the sink in my underwear, drinking a glass of cool tap water from a metal tumbler. It must be this: his presence infected you like a virus. Or was it just me? I felt lonely.

It was my childhood that had been lonely. We lived away from people and I had no siblings. I read a lot of books. There was a wild cat I tamed by leaving out little bowls of milk, and I talked to him in a soft voice while he lapped it up until he became used to me. The first time I tried to pet him he scratched me across the back of my hand, drawing blood; the wound became infected. The traces of it can still be seen on the back of my hand, the left, three pale lines. Somehow I wasn't deterred and continued to leave milk out for him, until he let me touch his neck and back, rub his face in my hands, and scratch his shoulder blades, finally carry him. I talked to him. We tramped out into the woods together, and I told him all the things I worried about. Quietly, because I didn't want anybody to hear. I had a sense, even then, that most things were secret. My family was that way. We had all been trained since birth to keep secrets, and we kept them well. While I was little, and still needed to speak, I could stuff it into the ears of the cat. Later, and for many years, I practiced silence. The tricky thing about silence is its weight, the heaviness it gives a particular word or name that sits unspoken on your tongue. That word or name may grow over time, filling your mouth, your lungs, your belly, with the evil and beauty of its absence. I have never met a person who has been able to bear the weight like I have. At least, nobody who could bear *my* weight, *my* silence. Relationships often ended before they began. Or, sometimes the middle lasted for months, but the end always came. It was not a question of fault or blame. It was just weight. It was alright, except for the times it wasn't.

But I was young. Sometimes I believed I was beautiful. I spent all my money on paint and canvas. I lived in the same tiny place I painted and breathed in the ferocious smell even as I slept. Though I never smoked, I loved to drink. I would stand in front of the mirror with a tumbler of pure gin in my hand and my lips parted, practicing a cocktail laugh. I would practice standing on the balls of my feet in high heels, walking from one end of the room to the other. Who or what was I practicing for? Dimly, I imagined some moment, some party, where my head would turn at the right angle, and I would laugh just right. Really, it had no purpose. I drank until my eyes got blurry and my body felt heavy and I would lie right down on the middle of my floor. This was the kind of drinking I did alone. In public, I kept to white wine, or beer, and only drank enough to feel it start. I may come home afterward and drink a little more. Or put on a song I liked and dance to it, or eat a piece of toast. It was a pleasure to get home after a party and turn on all the lights and take off my shoes and dance. Or to spill honey on a piece of bread spread thick with butter, to hold food in my mouth. Or taste the first spiky sip of real alcohol, gin or vodka. They were the secret pleasures of the body that animals must feel too. Sleep was a pleasure, falling asleep, in bed or on the floor. To let someone put their fingers or their cock inside me, to move warm against their skin. I was alone, sometimes, lonely, I had headaches—yes,

I felt, sometimes, desperate. But I couldn't deny my life held all the earthly pleasures any person could hope to expect.

The phone rang, it wasn't Krishna. It was my mother, or the landlord, or a friend or the phone company calling with an exclusive offer on long-distance rates. Why did I think—every time—it would be him? Why did I clear my throat and exhale in a little puff before I said hello?

It rained for weeks and weeks without stopping. My apartment got very hot and I had a dilemma about the windows: closed, the smell of my oils was too intense and made me dizzy, open, the water might blow in and spoil my paintings. I was sketching for a new piece that had to do with sound. I was interested in making something visual that mimicked the elemental experience of listening to music. I was interested in the affinities of light and noise, and felt very sure, for some reason, that I could create something new. Really what I was looking for was the moment that I met eyes with Krishna at that party, which was physical, and had weight and sound.

One of those mornings I woke up with a sudden craving for art and rushed to the museum to sit in front of the Rothko they have there. The room that contains the painting had no windows, only a sourceless constant light that seemed to deny the existence of day, night, cloud. I sat for awhile—who knows how long. It had a way of getting into me, the painting. The room filled and emptied several times. There were moments I felt as though I was falling in. The red and blue jangled against each other. Then the bench bent with new weight, and I looked beside me and saw Krishna. He was sitting very neatly like a cat that has gathered up all his paws, and wore quiet clothes: a checked blue shirt, and worn jeans and soft, leather boots. His skin seemed muted. It was storm blue—almost gray. His hair was in a braid down his back, a complicated pattern I had once tried and failed to master.

"What does it look like to you?" He had an ordinary, gentle voice, though once I'd heard it, I wondered what I had expected. The accent that shaded his vowels was unplaceable.

"Nothing," I said. "Just itself. Just colors."

"I thought it looked like a cupcake."

"You're probably hungry."

That amused him. "Yes, probably."

The space between us had opened, but in the small silence that followed, I could feel it starting to close again.

"Do you smoke?" I said.

"No—can't."

"Can't?"

"Shouldn't."

"Shouldn't. Well, who *should*?"

He tapped his finger to his lips. "You don't smoke either."

"How do you know?"

"I can smell it. Were you going to offer me a cigarette?"

"Yes."

"What would you have done if I accepted?"

"Well, I would have gone outside and patted all my pockets and pretended like I had forgotten I finished my pack."

"And then?"

"I didn't think that far. I may have gone to the corner store and bought some."

"And smoked one?"

"Yes. If we found a lighter."

I had been afraid to look at him. So close, I could smell sandalwood indistinctly, and something like juniper. I looked at the Rothko or his shoes. They were dark brown, worn, and had buckles instead of laces. But I could feel him quiet, smiling. It was easy. It was a dream of a friend.

"You were at that party."

"You remember?"

"I'm good with faces."

"Did you enjoy yourself?"

"Well—those parties—no. I'm tired of those parties."

"Why do you go?"

"People get so insulted. I don't know. I shouldn't." Then he sighed, and got to his feet. "I'm going to get a cupcake, would you like to come?"

"Yes," I said.

Krishna never dated, at least, the tabloids were never able to catch him in the middle of a romance. Everyone had questions about his body. Lady Baby claimed in an interview once that they'd slept together, and Krishna never dignified this allegation with a response. But the majority of rumors clustered around the world's most elite women, not tawdry pop stars: actresses and princesses, women who would never brag about their conquest or heartbreak. In my hot, tiny apartment, Krishna touched all my plants, and after his fingers left them their leaves seemed more green. Some water was caught in his hair from the rain outside, and my nose was running. We'd bought our cupcakes and eaten them wet on the street, in the rain. We took our wet shoes off, our wet socks. Krishna's toenails were just as pink as my own.

"Do you want something to drink? Some coffee?"

"Filter coffee?"

I smiled. "I can make it that way if you'd like."

I liked to watch him move around my apartment though it was messy, with clothes and books and shoes scattered across the floor. There were sketches everywhere, and many half-opened books, and plates that had the crusts of toast and tea bags sitting in a dirty circle of color.

"You draw?"

"I paint."

"Paint what?"

"Nothing. Shapes."

"Can I see?"

"Absolutely not."

Standing near the canvas, which I turned toward the wall when I was not working, I realized for the first time how small he really was, hardly any taller than me in bare feet. Up till now the glamour of his presence amplified him, but suddenly, for a single moment, the magic let up, and he seemed small and ordinary. Even the color of his skin, which seemed close to a human color, like brown.

"You don't show them at all?"

"Only when they're ready."

"Is this me?" He had picked up the newspaper where his face was drawn, which I hadn't thrown away. It gave me pleasure to look at, his eyes, his lips, though also shame. I could close my eyes at night and superimpose his face on the face that I had drawn, moving of its own volition, as my mind moved, turning back to him.

"Yes."

"Are you in love with me?"

I was so startled I didn't lie. "Yes."

"I can't love you."

"Can't—shouldn't—won't?"

He shook his head, and took the coffee when I gave it to him, cooled it by pouring it between two glasses. Then he stood by the window, taking it in neat sips. The city, in the rain, seemed insubstantial, the half-hazy cityscape of a dream. But he seemed real enough. I kept measuring his realness against things, him against the plants, him against the glass, him against the poster on the wall.

"I heard you painted too."

"From who?"

"I read about it. In the tabloids."

"You shouldn't read that garbage."

"Well, do you?"

"I dabble in a lot of things. I wouldn't call myself a painter."

"You studied with Keró."

"They said that in the tabloids?"

"No. Somewhere else, maybe, maybe an art magazine. Maybe someone told me."

"What do you really want to ask me?"

The question gave me permission to look at his face, right into his eyes. They were just eyes, brown eyes, like anyone could have, fringed with the heavy, curly lashes of a little boy. Yet, as I met them the sound passed through me again. And I whispered it, "Do you know me?" As soon as I said it, I felt frightened for the response. He touched my cheek with his fingers, cool and dry as leaves.

"No," he said. "How can I? We've just met."

That evening I sat with my glass in my hand in front of the mirror, and made myself cry. I had never seen myself cry and I was curious what I looked like. I had only seen the aftereffects—my red nose and eyes, the strange pinkness of my mouth—as I washed my face with cold water, trying to erase the signs of distress. When I normally cried, it was firmly into my pillow, with no sound, nearly breathless. What I wanted now was the whole thing: the formation of the tear, the heat building, the breath becoming ragged. I wanted the face covered in the gloss of tears and mucus, like a kind of oil. How to begin?

I took a sip of my drink. It warmed my throat and then my belly. I took another sip. I thought about my father, distance, my mother, my childhood home. But very quickly I saw that to think of these things stuffed everything up, my tears and my thoughts. I didn't feel sad so much as blank in the face of the memories. Hermetically sealed, sealed from myself. I tried again.

I thought of how one summer a girl my age had moved into a house down the street with her family. Corrie. She had warm, bright cheeks and a level gaze that trusted you; she was three months younger than me, born in winter. I encountered her one afternoon when my mother sent me to get the mail. She was standing in rubber boots down the street, so tiny I thought I'd imagined her. But she had seen me because she called out something, "Hey—" and in utter fright, I left the mail in the mailbox and ran back home. It was the same for three or four more days, and each day she came a little closer, until, by the fifth day, she was standing by my mailbox with an apple in her hand.

I had seen children before, of course. Sometimes I went into town with my mother to buy groceries or go to the doctor's or take tests. I was amazed by how they seemed to chatter on about nothing, how forcefully they asked for things, how easy they seemed in their surroundings, eating candy, talking to one another, so sure of the world and how it operated. It seemed absurd to me to ask for what I wanted, and I felt a kind of disdain for them, at least from a distance. But Corrie was real. She stood next to the mailbox, almost exactly as tall as it, and as tall as me, red-brown hair, and funny yellow eyes that could pass for brown in a certain light.

"You live here?"

"Yeah."

"We just moved there." She pointed. Her house was set back from the road, its blue sides showing in little gaps between the trees. We had watched it being built for almost a year, with nervous curiosity, waiting for the day the moving trucks would come in. "How old are you?"

"Nine."

"I'm eight and three-quarters. Do you want to know why I'm so small?"

"Why?"

"My mom said I was born premature. That means early. When I was a baby, they had to keep me in a little glass case like a princess in the hospital. When is your birthday?"

"August 15."

"Aren't you going to ask me what mine is?"

"No."

"Why not?"

"I don't know. Who cares?"

"It's polite."

"Why do you talk so much?"

She shrugged. "This is normal," she said. "This is how people talk."

I can remember her tiny body, her not-breasts. I could see her ribs through her skin like a horse. We slept in the same bed, in my bed, which was a loft, and very close to the ceiling. For a while, not talking, breathing. Speaking through breath. She had a mole on each of her cheeks that made her look grown-up. In the light, her face was blue, her skin.

"What color is your vagina?"

"What?"

"Your vagina?"

"What is that?"

She pointed. "What do you call it?"

"Nothing."

"It's probably a different color."

"I've never looked. What color is yours?"

"Pink, I guess. I can't see if I look myself."

"Should I look?"

"Okay."

I had a sense we were moving into a secret place, and the thought both alarmed me and gave me comfort. I knew how to tongue a secret quietly for hours, pulling at its sweet-sourness like a hard candy. She sat up, her head nearly touching the ceiling, and switched on the flashlight we had brought into bed with us, to read under the covers with. She dangled her legs off the side of the bed as she pulled down her shorts, then her underpants, and lifted her shirt awkwardly, wrestling her head out of it, then sat, small and pale and naked on my bed, swinging her legs, just next to the beam of the flashlight, which made a cool yellow circle on the wall behind.

"Lie down," I said.

She lay.

"Pretend you're dead."

"Okay." She closed her eyes. I brought my face close to her belly and smelled her skin: like bread before it's baked. And the smell I look for in lovers now, groping for it with only a half-sense that I'm looking for anything at all: the soft, human smell of skin, sweat, scalp, scent of the body's work and movement through the day, that smell that is the scent of time accruing on the skin, that cannot be erased by a bath or a hot shower.

Skin met skin and I pressed it open with my fingers. Under the light it was a pure, dull pink, like the inside of a shell. I felt a spike of feeling, which I thought was disgust, and withdrew my hand quickly. She had let out a sigh.

"Your turn."

"You're dead."

"Now you are. What color was it?"

"Like you said. Pink."

I lay on my back to feel it, the coolness of death coming over me like cold air. She pulled a lip indelicately between her fingers, as though inspecting it for defects, and the feeling spiked up again, more secret. This time it was physical, the feeling. The weight of it made me gasp. I was as happy and frightened as a firework might be. Her fingers were cold.

Her voice had shock, "Oh, it's ugly," she said, "It's purple."

"Purple?"

"Brown. Brown or purple."

I leaned up on my elbows and she shone the light in my face.

"Like your lips."

"You're lying," I said.

"No I'm not," she said, keeping the light in my face, where it dazzled my eyes. I could see her through that film of light, just in outline. But her voice wasn't cruel, only factual. "Your lips aren't ugly, but your vagina is."

"Yours is too," I spat, and bumped my head on the ceiling as I sat up, because I wasn't being careful.

Now, in the mirror, I examined myself. My eyes were dry, but my face looked slightly wild. I took a beautiful swallow of the drink, ending it, then poured myself another. Memory clearly wouldn't help. But I remembered a scene that had passed outside my window three days ago, of a man in the crosswalk who had dropped a sheaf of papers and had to kneel to pick them back up, growing more desperate as the light turned from green to yellow, not knowing whether to stay in the crosswalk and keep gathering his papers or to retreat to the sidewalk and watch them scatter across the busy street in the wind, where they would be impossible to retrieve. I remembered the look on his face in the green to yellow moment. And finally at the very last second he picked himself up and walked to the curb, shaking his head.

I felt the tears start seconds before they became apparent, pricking at the inside corners of my eyes. Then the whole rim of my eyes filled and brimmed over, like too much water pouring into a glass, but unevenly, my left eye filling more quickly than my right. I watched my eyes redden. My lips were curled up, almost snarling, showing teeth. The heat in my face. Drinking, I loved myself, this face I had never seen. Drinking, and crying into my drink, not with sadness. Not with sadness I was sure. Either I didn't have the vocabulary to express what I felt, or the word did not exist: it was a color, blue. But say the word blue and everyone thinks something different. I went to the bathroom and blew my nose into a towel.

"Mother, I've met Krishna!"

But I never made that call. I thought of it all the time. I didn't tell anyone.

When I began painting the new canvas my days took on a particular and constant rhythm. I would wake in the morning with a bad headache and make a cup of filter coffee with lots of sugar. While I waited for it to cool I would eat a bowl of cereal, change into my work clothes and sit at the canvas for a while, mentally painting what I would physically paint during the day. I worked from an elaborate sketch I had made a few weeks before. I blocked out the canvas into fields of color; within these fields, I saw the lines as finely as ant-work, and before long I was reaching for my smallest brushes, squinting hard at the tiny movements of color. Around one or two I'd get very hungry, and eat the same cheese sandwich every day, and then work until dusk. Sometimes I would skip dinner for drinks, and turn the television on, not to be entertained, but rather to have something to ignore. I had only a few months more before my fellowship ran out, and I spent my money on rent, paint, and liquor, leaving the house infrequently except to replenish my supply of the latter two.

During this time I was asked to three parties and went to all of them. One was given by some people I had known in art school, and who had the most beautiful tattoos of anyone on earth, where I drank more than I had meant to and kissed more people than I remembered, and took one of them home and let him come inside me without a condom, because at that moment, helplessly, I had wanted it, more than anything I had wanted it. In the morning I went to the drugstore with a blinding headache to get the pill I needed to take, and then took it, swallowing with my own spit right there in the drugstore because I didn't want to waste time. The second and third party were both given by friends of the friend of a friend, in impossibly beautiful houses, with carpets that felt, if you walked on them barefoot, as though you were walking through soft fine grass. At both of these parties I didn't drink too much and looked at each person with desperate hope as they walked through the door, but they were never Krishna. He was nowhere. In the papers there was a sudden silence about him, even the tabloids.

"You're thin," said Krishna, sitting on the exact middle step of the carpeted staircase that led up to my apartment.

The seventh. I was so surprised to see him I nearly dropped the bag I was carrying, full of breakables. It was March, unseasonably cold, and I was wearing a hat over my neglected hair, and my coat was dirty and I smelled. The wind had slammed the lobby door shut behind me.

"Thank you."

"I'm not encouraging you." Blue as figs in a still life, in a T-shirt and jeans and sneakers like a twenty-year-old boy, and a big soft hat that hid all his hair. "Do you need help?"

"No," I said. I shifted the bags in my arms. "Come in."

Entering with him, I noticed the smell of my apartment, the dense harsh smell of color that comforted me but might choke him. It was clear out but cold: I opened the windows, and clicked on the stove without asking and started to make him coffee. He took off his shoes and sunglasses and inspected, as he had the first time, picking up the sketches I had left lying around. It was too late to try and gather up the dirty clothes that were everywhere, so I just let him look.

"You've been working?"

"Yes."

"Can I see?"

"No."

He slid his hat off. Underneath, the hair was gone, only a thin, soft-looking fur close to the scalp.

"What happened?"

"Nothing. I cut it."

"It was so beautiful."

He shrugged. "It grows."

"Where have you been?"

"What did your tabloids say?"

"They haven't said anything about you." Then I blushed, I knew I shouldn't still be reading them. But how else was I to know?

"I have a gift for you."

"You do?"

His hand dipped into his pants pocket, and reappeared with a flat blue bead. His palm, extended, was peach-pink, and there was a line on the sides that sharply delineated the pink from blue.

"It's sea-glass."

I took it and tucked it in my cheek. It was cool, and strangely sweet.

"Where were you?"

"Oh, many places. I went home for a while."

"Mathura?"

"No, that's where I was born. I live in Kerala. Well, I have a house there."

"What did you do there?"

"Nothing. I was quiet. I just stayed quiet for awhile."

"I've been to Mathura once."

"Oh yes?"

"Yes, when I was younger. It was cold there. Everyone wore shawls around their head at the train station."

"Aren't you going to put your groceries away?"

"I'll do it later."

"Do it now."

"Why?"

He sat down at my little table. "Are you ashamed of something?"

"Everyone's ashamed of something."

I poured his coffee. His straight blue fingers tapped on the white table.

"I'm not."

"Nothing?"

"No."

"That must be nice for you."

"It's a choice."

"I didn't ask for advice."

"I'm not giving it."

I sat down with him at the table, on the other side of the same corner, to look at him without looking at him too openly, able, at least, to see the stubble on his cheek that looked a day or two old, glinting in the light that came in from the window. He picked up the glass and poured back and forth, in a way that struck me as showy, pulling the glasses farther and farther apart while the brown ribbon of coffee thinned but never broke.

"What's Kerala like?"

"You've never been?"

"No."

"You should come visit me there."

"What's it like?"

"It's very beautiful, very green. It's good for you to breathe in that kind of air. Thick, hot. It's so thick it seems liquid; it's full of smell. In the summers it's almost unbearable. But during winter—"

He paused for a moment.

"What?"

"You're distracted. You're not here."

"I'm here. Summer . . . winter . . ."

"I can see your thoughts just drifting along."

"You can *see* my *thoughts*?"

"Not literally."

"Figuratively."

"Yes."

"What do my thoughts look like? Figuratively?"

He rubbed his hands across his head. The hair was so feathery short that through it I could see a black-blue birthmark behind his left ear, kidney-shaped. It had smooth edges, nicely formed, the curve of it echoing the larger curve of his ear, as though someone had drawn it there, placed it purposefully, to make his smooth head slightly imperfect. But it was a perfect imperfection. It angered me.

"Just pale, thin, one after the other, anemic-looking. Blurry."

"My thoughts are anemic?"

"Don't get muddled up in words," he said kindly. "You know what I mean, don't you? Close your eyes."

I closed them.

"What are you thinking about?"

"I don't know."

"Okay, don't say them aloud. Just name them as they pass."

Krishna's birthmark, gin, gin, my mother's face when she was cooking. Krishna's slender wrists. My painting, those little faces, the little eyes. Gin. The first sip of gin I ever took, thirteen, spat it out on the kitchen floor. The smell of alcohol is similar to the smell of paint. Painting has the word *pain* in it, and your arms do ache after a while, your wrists. His wrists look delicate enough to snap in half.

"You see now?"

"But I paint."

"You paint."

"Painting takes strength, strong thoughts."

"You use it all up for art and then there is nothing left over."

"Good. I want to spend my whole life on art."

"You don't have to, and anyway you can't."

"What do you know about it?"

"Nothing," he said. His face stayed quite calm, though anger was leaking into mine, I could feel it rising in my cheeks. "Don't listen to me if you think I'm wrong."

"People's thoughts don't look like anything. It's a party trick."

"What's in the bag?"

"You tell me. You seem to know anyway."

"Gin," he said. "Three bottles of gin, and one bottle of vodka. You want me to leave so you can have some."

"No."

"No? Three bottles of vodka, one bottle of gin?"

"No. I don't want you to leave."

He put his hat back on.

"Poor little human," he said.

In a dream, Krishna called me to Kerala. His house was permeated with the outdoors, and filled with thick air and wandering animals. Peacocks with their cat-like cries, and leopards, and ground-snakes and iridescent insects and jack-als and mongoose, I walked through room after room, each space humble in the clean white cotton of a mourner. In the middle of a wide white bed Krishna lay half covered by a cotton sheet, a blue marble disappearing into a glass of milk. His chest was bare and smooth as the still surface of a lake.

"Krishna?"

His eyes came open. The same brown eyes I had seen in waking life, not altered by the dream-state. "I'm glad you came."

I was in bed with him. We lay, not touching, both naked, under the sheet. I lifted the sheet and ducked my head under to look at the beautiful length of him, strong and compact as a fighter.

"Is it true you had a thousand wives?"

"Did your tabloids tell you that too?"

"No. My mother told me. She said the one you loved

the most you never married. And the rest you had to marry for political reasons."

"What do you think?"

"I think that if it's true you have a real hard time saying no."

He laughed.

"Can I ask you something else?"

"Of course."

"Can I look inside your mouth?"

He came close to me. I could feel the heat of him so close. So close but he wouldn't yet touch me. I could smell him, the sandalwood, the juniper, the absence of that mortal smell I was always able to find on the skin of my lovers.

"Please," I said. And then I added, with desperate sadness, "I know this is just a dream."

He took hold of me, I felt his skin around me, strangely cool to the touch like embracing water, as he pushed inside me, like water flooding through the core, the odd buoyancy of Dead Sea water, dry-cool, stunning, moving through me again and again. His face was folded in concentration, gentle, as though he was praying. An ugly nest of scars was stuck on his right shoulder, a palm-shaped wound that looked as though it had never quite healed. I brushed my fingers over it. His blood was right there, separated from mine by just two thin layers of skin. When our two faces were lined up, his over mine, he closed his eyes and, as though he were about to sing or scream, opened his mouth.

Yes, I saw there what I'd known I would see: the three worlds suspended in darkness, each one glowing like a star.

I saw a girl who looked like Corrie at the far away grocery store that had the cheaper booze and followed her from one aisle to the next. It was Thursday evening. At first I was following her to be sure it was actually her, but in the snack aisle I determined it was from the way she moved, which had the same clumsy friendliness that she had approached me with all those years ago, though she had grown lean, and I only dared to look at her face in profile, and could therefore only see one of her two symmetrical moles. The last time I had seen her was in high school. Her family had moved back into town and mine had decided to send me to school for my last three years because they were tired of homeschool, maybe, or maybe because my dad changed jobs and had to work in an office instead of from home, so he could drive me on his way there. Nothing good came of that decision, of course. A city girl airlifted into the Alaskan wild couldn't have done worse than I did at lunch, or in gym class, in those horrible shorts. Corrie didn't know me anymore—she erased me, and I didn't blame her. When I looked at her, she was always looking the other way. It seemed as though, when we met together as kids in those afternoon acts, we had each proven our essential nature: a sort of radiant wholeness in Corrie, sleekly chubby with adolescence, and an ugly misalignment in me, my teenage body a jumble of sullen angles.

"Corrie?" I had to repeat the name before the girl turned. Tight jeans, tight jacket, sneakers, all black. And she was thin, sharply thin, and pretty, with clear, flawless skin. But there was no matching mole on the other cheek, and the elements of her face resolved themselves entirely differently when I looked at her full on.

"I'm sorry, I thought you were this girl I went to high school with."

She shrugged. "Maybe I am. I went to a big school."

"But your name's not Corrie."

"No."

"What is it then?"

"Athalie."

"I've never heard it before."

"It's French. My mother's French."

"It's funny, you have a mole—just right where she had one. Right here." I touched my left cheek to mirror her right.

"Oh this?" She smiled. "I draw it on."

"You do? Why?"

"You know—a beauty spot. You put an imperfection on your face to make it seem more perfect. My mother—" She stopped, blushed. "Well."

"It is perfect. Your face. Everything is symmetrical about it. It's perfectly aligned."

"Just genes," she said. "Are you hitting on me?"

"I think I am," I said.

It was seven, evening, but like the museum, the grocery

store was windowless and was lit by its own white-blue light. And I had found Corrie. Her slim girl-hips and her newly lean face. I wanted to put my hands around her. She was shorter than me now and seemed more fragile. I had brushed my teeth before I left so my breath wouldn't smell too boozy, though I had only expected to talk to a cashier.

"Are you having a party?" said Athalie, looking at my basket full of bottles.

"Yes, do you want to come?"

"When is it?"

"This weekend."

"Okay," she said. I couldn't tell if she believed me.

"Can I walk you home?"

"—picked me up at a grocery store, I mean, I've never done anything like this, I'm telling you—"

I heard my voice say, very quietly, "Corrie?"

Then her face was there, above mine, almost, almost her face. The mole on her left cheek was smudged, no, my right so her left, smudged, and her swan's neck bare, her breasts bare, naked, all of her, her naked feet. Not Corrie. Why did I think of Corrie anymore? "Not Corrie. I didn't even like Corrie. Athalie."

"I don't know your name."

"Radika."

"Radika. Sounds like a hiccup."

I could taste the cigarettes in her mouth. I sat on a blue couch. Naked on a blue couch. Hot-cold. Thighs splayed out against the rough fabric, my strange little belly and my breasts, the blue bead Krishna gave me suspended between, hanging on a loop of mint flavored dental floss. Corrie was more beautiful. Lust parted her lips. Wet taste of cigarettes.

"Can I put the mole on your other cheek?"

"You want me to look like that girl."

"Yes—do you mind?"

"Do you think I'm pretty?"

"Pretty? No, no. That word doesn't mean anything when I look at you. The shape, and color of you—like if a flower was a creature, that's you. Athalie. Soft, and bright and love-ly."

Corrie with a mole on each cheek. Those honey-colored eyes that make you want to tongue the iris. Returning to the places she has touched. Her shell-pink nipples and tongue. Helpless in my shameful pleasure: *Corrie—I'm sorry—*

Where had I been? What had happened? I thought I saw Krishna, but after a little while I knew I hadn't, like a wish given momentary form, it had been another person wearing, just for a second, his body. I slept and woke and stood up in my clothes, smelly, and the room tilted and righted several times. It was like walking in an earthquake, or on water. I made it to the bathroom and threw up in the toilet.

Not my toilet. The tiles in this bathroom were blue. The towels were clean, and beautiful. At the sink there was shell-shaped soap. The mirror contained a surprised face. The skin was sallow in the reflected blue light, my bloodshot eyes.

It was a beautiful, sunlit apartment. For a moment I almost couldn't see through the pain that light brought. Then, my eyes focused, a couch, an open door, an unmade bed, a note on the kitchen table, next to a wooden bowl full of lemons. I picked one up and held it to my face, smelling it, tasting the bright color with my eyes, as though it would wake me. Then I dressed and washed my face in the sink and left the apartment. I could hear the door lock behind me. I stood in front of the building just to get my bearings.

What street, what day—what was my name? That came first. When I held the syllables in my mouth I was able to sift through the streets of the city in my mind, and place myself. I began to walk. My mouth was dry. What had happened? I pressed my mind against the memory of last night. Light, light, light was falling around me like rain. I pulled a name out: Corrie. I got right to the edge of the memory. Then I decided I didn't want to remember and turned my mind away.

At home, I stripped my clothes off and took a purely hot shower, and felt myself returning. By the time I was finished, I was almost cured. I made and drank a cup of simple coffee, in my underwear, gagged down a bowl of cereal, and dressed in my work clothes. I was good at ignoring headaches. In fact, often the things I hated about being hungover were the things I liked about it too: the constant reminder that you are alive, in possession of a body. Your head said, "head." Your belly said, "belly." And your mind was squeezed out of it.

Drinking could help you along, of course, but I never did it on a workday, a morning when I was painting, which was every morning, even Sundays: I had been very strict about that rule. Because the work was so finely detailed, I knew I needed my fingers smart and limber. Today though, it had nothing to do with my head saying "head" and my belly saying "belly." It was only this: I wanted the taste of it. For no other reason than it would taste nice. It would feel very nice on my tongue and going down my throat. Not to get drunk, of course not. It took a lot to get drunk anyway. Just to have the taste in my mouth to move me along as I worked.

I had forgotten the bottles I had bought last night at the apartment I had woken up in: no matter. I was being proactive. I used to keep beer or wine in the fridge before I realized it was a waste of money and after that I only bought spirits. On a high shelf in the kitchen I kept a reserve bottle of vodka for emergencies, I think the way people keep guns, for comfort.

This morning I knew I had to keep working, but I was only going to have a taste. I knew this as I climbed up on the counter to reach the high shelf, and the bottle was cool in my hands as I pulled it down, a little friendly gentleman, Russian, with a smart blue cap. I felt, all of a sudden, quite cheerful. The sound that the cap made as I twisted it off was crisp, like a fresh carrot snapped in half. There was no need to dirty a glass, so I put my lips to the bottle. The moment before the liquid passed through my lips and touched my tongue, I had no thoughts. Not one. My body, hungry, open, reaching, was singular in its focus. It was a state like praying.

Five sips, then I climbed up and put the bottle back. I felt good: clearer, steadier. I stood at my canvas and looked at it. It felt quite large to me, and there was so much work to do. I took my palette from the fridge and darkened a brush with color, almost arbitrarily. Then I stood in front of the canvas again. Just looked at it. I began to feel that ugly thing for my project that I had somehow miraculously evaded up till now: doubt. So much work—for what? Of a seven by ten foot canvas, I had completed only one little corner. Who would see it? Who would want it? Who would care?

It was like standing at a podium and clearing your throat again and again instead of speaking. I stood there for an hour, maybe longer, unable to work, unable to quit, just stood there. I had to go right down to the core of myself and touch it before I could put any more color to that canvas. And even after that, the work was slow. But I worked. I could say that for myself, painting took strength, and I was strong. If my mind wandered, it wandered, I brought it back, as I always did.

That time I lost some hours but not a whole day.

When I saw Krishna next, if I saw him again, I would show him. It wasn't finished, but I would show him anyway. Just to prove that my thoughts were strong. If he saw my paintings there wouldn't be any doubt. He might love me. He might leave me alone.

But mornings. The hammer worked at me and I woke dry and brittle, or already smashed into pieces. It took longer to put the pieces together. I lay in bed for many minutes or hours. Part of me talked to the other, tired part, murmuring at it almost kindly, but after a while it would change tactics and my mind would begin to berate itself. What an incredible store of insults it had to draw on. I could very nearly see my father's face as he unbuckled his belt. I put my feet on the floor. Good. I went to the bathroom and brushed my teeth. I made coffee black and drank it, several cups. No need for breakfast after that. I put on my work clothes.

And then, the slipping. I could see it happen before it did. But I needed something, some courage. I climbed up and brought the bottle down. I stood it alone on the counter. Looked at it. Some days the sight of the bottle was the most beautiful thing I would look at all day. Rectangular with rounded corners, the lettering was in big, blocky letters, that jaunty blue cap. The liquid in it was entirely clear, just like any piece of the sky would be, if you separated it from the rest. First just a smell, bracing, with my nose to the mouth of the bottle. Then the small beautiful first taste, like a door opening. Then there was a second taste. Then I would put the bottle down. I may even go so far as to put the bottle back on its shelf. I would pop the blue bead into my mouth and suck it as though it were a candy necklace. But the thought of Krishna often made me ashamed. I spat the blue bead out and let it dry against my chest. I climbed back up and took another few swallows standing on the counter. Put it back in the cabinet. Climbed back down. Stood with my hands braced against the counter, with my eyes closed. There was the perfect state in which I could still paint, that dulled me but didn't make me sloppy. I could still paint and I was happy. I felt truly happy. But not enough alcohol and I would feel itchy, physically itchy to drink more. And too much made me want to lie down on the floor and watch the sun slide across the ceiling until noon or later. It was the difference between two shots and three, or three shots and four, or the difference between nine sips and ten, or nine little sips then one big sip and ten normal sized sips. I found the state often, but only too late, after I had already drunk more and was only able to pass through it. Like being on a train that would slow down but not stop at your station, and you were late, and in a panic you would watch the station go by. I tried to keep track of the magic number, but it was a shifting target: one day the amount I drank sent me into a stupor, the next day it was not even enough to get me drunk.

I lost many days.

I found myself one afternoon at a park; I had an idea that I had wanted to be around people, not to talk to them, but just to be near them, and to see their faces. It had gotten warm. I sat down in the grass. It was nice to feel the sun on my arms and the grass itching against my legs and palms. There was a couple sitting on a blanket and I sat down behind them, just to hear them speak. From where I was sitting I couldn't see their faces, only the way their bodies turned to each other, like matching parentheses. The man with his hand in the woman's black hair. I didn't want that man—or any man's—hands in my hair. Just to hear her voice moving above the sounds that children made on the playset, the tinny music projected from a cellphone some feet away, the bird chatter that rose like mist from the ground and the trees. To know that on this afternoon a man and a woman sat in a park and talked about her mother.

After a while they lay on their backs on the blanket and dozed. Three separate enterprising people offered to sell me a weed cookie, or a weed brownie, or a sandwich made with weed hummus, all of which I declined. Each time a person approached me it was a shock to remember that I existed in the human world, along with everyone else. I didn't feel like a human at all. I felt like a dog that sniffs around and eats pizza crusts he finds in the trash. Or, less: a bird and her crumb. Or maybe I was the worm.

It was evening when I woke up from the chill and walked home. The fog was coming in. In my mouth, a metallic taste hummed, and my body felt strangely heavy. When I got home, I realized that all of my plants were dead, all but one: a scrappy fern that was holding on for dear life. I stroked his yellowing leaves with my thumb. I took him to the sink and ran the tap over him to wet down his soil and let the water drain through. The rest I couldn't look at.

I have strong thoughts.
   I have *strong thoughts.*
      I have strong thoughts.

My hands shook. They were lazy, distracted, like two toddlers who didn't listen to their mother. Big, square hands, ill-suited to the delicate work I asked from them. They wandered. They weren't mine.

In front of the Rothko I sat and sat. It had never looked more beautiful to me. It existed outside of space, time, pain, and longing. It was just itself, just color. Blue and red, and the color they made when they touched. If I could understand it—I felt like I must. I sat there and tried and tried to understand it. At the same time it was clear to me that there was nothing to understand. It had nothing to explain and needed no explanation. Yet I felt like I must say something for it. My mind twisted itself against the problem, knotting tighter and tighter, and I began to cry. I was not sad, only tired of not knowing. Rothko was gone and could say nothing now, and even if he could, he may not know the answer himself. In fact, I knew even he wouldn't know, because there was no one, no answer. There wasn't even any question.

I felt a gentle hand on the small of my back and started. I thought it was the guard, who eyed me wearily as I entered the gallery, come to ask me to leave. But it was Krishna.

"I thought I might find you here."

"Were you looking for me?"

"You were looking for me."

I wiped my face with the sleeve of my sweatshirt. "I don't want a riddle right now."

"What do you want, Radika?"

I shook my head.

"Have you ever been to the Rothko Chapel in Houston?"

"No."

"You'd like it so much. It's a very clean, simple space. A person can feel very quiet there."

"Yeah, but you're in Houston."

"Some people can even feel quiet in Houston," he said. I didn't want to look at him; I didn't want to see myself reflected in his face. I wanted to delay that moment for as long as I could. I didn't know exactly what I would see there, but it would be one of two colors, pity or disgust, or some blend. I saw this color on so many faces now, as they passed me, if they saw me, and I didn't want to see it on his. "There are skylights that sort of diffuse the light over the paintings. The paintings change as the light moves. Imagine it. Light paints them, and cloud. They exist in the world and outside of it."

"Rothko died, didn't he? He killed himself before the chapel was finished. How peaceful could it be?"

"It's different from this one. There's nothing violent about it. He doesn't distract you with color. He's not asking."

"I've seen pictures."

"Pictures aren't enough sometimes. You should go."

"Okay, I'll go. Someday I'll go. Happy?"

Very quietly, he said my name. The same way a mother said "sweet pea" to her kid. But I didn't want his gentleness: didn't need it, didn't ask for it, didn't deserve it, couldn't use it. It was like a birthday gift for a dead girl. I got up and began to walk away, and I knew he was following me though I couldn't hear his cat steps. I walked down the huge granite staircase that always felt to me like the staircase of an Egyptian tomb. Then I began to run. I ran across the lobby and pushed the door open. It was cold outside, and the street was crowded. Where was I running? I crossed the street and stopped. I was standing in front of a fountain that spurted cold, dirty water. I sat down on the ledge of it and stuck my fingers in. I was waiting for Krishna to come, and he came, and sat down beside me. I took those deep, jagged breaths until I was calmer. Then I was calm. I looked at him. He was wearing saffron: cotton T-shirt, colored jeans. He was the most vivid blue I had ever seen.

WEDDING SEASON

THE BITTER SMELL of the mosquito coil woke her, just before dawn. Tejas had not slept deeply. But Al was already up, standing at the dark window.

"What time is it?"

"Five o' seven," said Al. She was wearing her flannel pajamas, which looked so out of place here. The walls were painted a sick green and it was cold. Through the window, Tejas could see the city's rooftops, shining flatly with the last of the moon.

"Why didn't the alarm go off?"

"Broken maybe."

"You should have woken me up."

"We slept bad last night," said Al, and shrugged. She sat down on the bed. Her hair was rough and gold, even in this light, as Tejas's eyes adjusted. She was wearing a gray wool sweater, which itched Tejas's bare arms as she held her and kissed the top of her head.

"Your hair's sticking straight up in the back," said

Al, smiling, and put her fingers in it to smooth it. "You hungry?"

"It's too early."

"Me neither."

They dressed and left the room. The rickshaw dropped them at the north gate, from there they had to walk. Dawn was rising over the city, the sky was pink with it through all the pollution. It smelled, even here, like rubber burning. A man followed them with a basket full of snow globes, called after them down the long gravel path though they didn't heed him, and kept walking with a deliberate quietness. He held one out to them, and called to them as they bought their tickets, a little plastic dome with a model of the Taj inside, chips of whirling glitter. Then they passed through the gate and the gardens and were rid of him. Early, but still a crowd was gathered. The sound of the morning call to prayer spread thinly out.

"It doesn't even snow here," said Al.

"People will buy anything, I guess." Tejas said. She examined Al, standing with a hand on her hip. Her hair was in a ponytail, and she was wearing jeans and that rough sweater. The color had come into her cheeks. She looked like a farm girl. "If you sell it hard enough."

They hung around, at that gate, for a few minutes, then went in. It wasn't as beautiful as Tejas remembered. She had remembered the feeling of walking through a dream, being lifted out of herself. Here, she felt ordinary, was ordinary. Al took a picture with her digital camera, examined the screen, frowned, and deleted it. By the time they left it was mid-morning, and the crowd had swelled. Still, the same vendor who had followed them on the way in remembered them, and called out to them again. He shook a globe in his hand. Tejas wanted to say something nasty to him in Hindi, and began to prepare the words on her tongue. But Al turned to him, and put her hand out. "How much?" she said.

"Three hundred for you, madam."

Al went to her money belt, and counted it out.

"He's ripping you off," Tejas hissed.

"It's okay," said Al. She gave him the money.

"Why encourage him?"

"I want it," said Al.

The man handed her the snow globe. He had beautiful hands, pink palms, thin wrists, expressive hands. She tried to look at his face, his eyes, to find a clue of what his life may be like. Agra was a desolate city, they had found, killing time when they arrived the day before but couldn't yet check in at the hotel. The landscape was gray and strangely industrial, and they had strayed into a part of town that seemed to regard them with suspicion. They kept a steady stream of banal conversation up between them, which grew more desperate as time went by. They had reached the end of the world, here, cold and dusty. Tejas felt she was losing the thread of herself.

Nothing in the man's eyes gave him away. He didn't smile, met her gaze evenly, didn't flinch, didn't turn lascivious. He was a good man, thought Tejas suddenly. Al shook the snow globe in her hands as they walked away, the water frothing at the top, the shards of glitter spinning crazily, nothing like snow, anyway.

In Goa they lived for a week in a little hut, right on the beach. It was deserted this time of year, close to the rains, they could feel it gathering. The air they moved through was hot and thick, had a physical weight, pushing against them like gravity. The beauty of it: they could hold hands, kiss if they wanted to, there was no one to see them, and perhaps no one would have suspected them even if they saw. Still, they were cautious. Tejas waded into the water while Al stayed onshore. The water was thick with salt, and soft, luxuriously so, like bedsheets for the rich. She was wearing a one-piece, modestly cut. She looked out at the shore, where Al was. She wore a skirt over her swimsuit and had taken her shoes off. They were separated by ten, maybe fifteen feet, but Tejas could see the ten flicks of color on the points of her feet, orange. A few paces away, a cow curled up like a dog and slept in the sand. The palm trees at the shore all leaned in toward the sea. Tejas waved at Al. "Why don't you come in?" she called.

"Later," said Al. She pointed at the things they had brought, their money belts and books and sunscreen and the keys to their little hut.

"There's no one here."

"Better to be careful."

Tejas nodded. For a minute, facing out to sea, she was alone on all sides. The ocean felt different from the Pacific, more forgiving, and the air was thicker than back home. Almost like she was dreaming, as she dove in, feeling alone, and the water against her. She closed her eyes and moved in it, kneeling in it, wetting her hair. The water was so beautifully warm she felt as though she were dancing in it, and knelt again, bobbed up, laughing, alone. Like a creature moving, moving by instinct. Blind against the water, she knelt again, dove down into it, the shallow tide. The pure, hollow space of herself was filled with nothing, not even worry.

She wiped the salt out of her eyes and looked back at Al. A group of local boys had appeared some ways off, kicking a soccer ball between them. Al watched them with interest. They were all teenagers, the boys, wearing shirts and shorts and no shoes, skinny calved. One would kick the ball into the surf, and the waves would wash it back out. A massive kick and they ran, moving brightly, bounding like dogs.

Al was up. She had met the ball, and kicked it back to them. The boys gave out a cry of surprise, and pleasure, the waves swallowed their words, but the tone Tejas could hear, and the edges of Al's laughter. Then they absorbed her into the game.

Tejas left the water. She sat on the shore and dried herself, rubbing her arms down too hard, and when Al returned to her, laughing and sweating, Tejas took her polished foot in her hand and pressed it.

"You left our stuff."

"I didn't go very far."

"They could have robbed us."

"Don't," she said, and tugging her foot away.

"My other cousin married a white girl."

"That's different, though, isn't it?"

"Maybe. Anyway, he was on my dad's side."

They lay in bed, long after dark, with the mosquito netting around them. There was a dog barking, the hum of the fan, and the swooping, eerie call of some night bird. In the dark, Al's legs showed blueish white.

"Can I confess something to you?"

"Yes, of course."

"I used to watch straight porn. Does that gross you out?"

"Did you like it?"

"I don't know," said Al. "Sort of, I guess."

"It doesn't gross me out," said Tejas. "Bertie?"

"Yes?"

"Will you tell me you don't love me anymore?"

"Why?"

"I don't know. I just have this feeling, like I want to hear you say it."

"But it's not true."

"I know it's not."

The fan switched off, and the light shining in from the yard out front went dark. The room became hot and still.

Tejas was lying on her side, facing away from Al. All at once the dogs were barking in a frenzy outside.

"Again?" said Al. "They're really going to get us now."

"There's the net."

"There's holes in it."

"They like me more," said Tejas. "Anyway, would you say it?"

"I don't know why you want me to."

"Bertie," said Tejas, "please?"

"Alright," said Al. Tejas could hear her inhale as she sat up. "I don't love you anymore. Okay?"

"Okay," said Tejas. She tried it on. It felt worse than she imagined. "Okay."

"You're feeling sorry for yourself," said Al, wonderingly.

Tejas had fallen in love with Al quite suddenly, and noticed it only one morning before she was about to leave for work. It was raining outside, and Al was drinking from a mug of half-coffee, half-milk at her kitchen table, reading a three-day-old newspaper. She went to work later than Tejas, and had slow, warm mornings that Tejas envied from the start, though she came home later and more tired than Tejas too. It was nothing, a smile, as she glanced up from the page.

"You're going to bike?"

"I guess so. Otherwise I'll be late."

"Be careful." Then she said, "What?"

"What what?"

"You're looking at me funny."

Tejas felt uncontrollably shy and looked at her feet. "Nothing," she said. Two weeks later, it was Al who held her close while they were dancing, pressing her damp cheek to Tejas' own, and shouting the three good syllables in her ear.

Walking together became normal, holding hands. Al stood up straighter and moved through a crowd like a blade, pulling Tejas through. They were in the park for a free concert, and Tejas took off her shoes, the grass crushed cool under her feet. The music moved her. On stage, a man playing the evening ragas of her babyhood. He held the long instrument against his body, moving his fingers quickly up and down the neck. Al's fingers moved in unconscious sympathy with the musician's. How solidly she stood on the ground, never resisting. "You like it?"

"I like it!"

Eyes filled with each other. Love, perhaps, not a feeling, but a way of looking. Flooding open.

Bombay was hot, and thickly moist, dusty, crowded, and endless. It was impossible to get a grasp on time and space. You could spend an hour pushing through just a single mile of the city, fall off the map and spend hours trying to find your way back on it, suddenly it was dark, and the dogs followed you hopefully, and little kids too. Deeper and deeper the road ran, into what felt like a village, where shacks with open doors showed rooms lit in harsh fluorescent and the flicker of the TV, and mosques leaked prayer into the hot night. Their entourage had fallen away, and there was no way out but to retrace their steps: the night gave them a sense of anonymity and a piercing sense of aloneness that was not unpleasant. They found their way back to a busy road, and hailed a rickshaw, which took them home.

Three days until her cousin's wedding, and the whole family was too busy to show them around, which was just as well. At other times, Tejas had been passed around from aunt to cousin to distant cousin, never allowed to handle money or direct the day, often left for hours in rooms full of relatives who talked rapidly in a language she did not speak. The wandering with Al felt illicit and dangerous, though Al seemed oblivious to it.

At night, they slept in the only bedroom in her aunt and uncle's flat, while her aunt and uncle slept on the floor and sofa in the living room, respectively: no persuading them otherwise. The air conditioning was on, and the sounds from the street came in, even this high up, the endless fire-crackers from the political rallies, day and night.

"I feel like I've smoked three packs of cigarettes," Al said, whispering on instinct. Tejas felt tired, but her mind was buzzing. She kept her body against Al's nervously, wondering what it would look like to her family if they came in. She had her arms around her, and her nose and cheek pressed to her hair. Did sisters sleep like this?

"Delhi's worse."

"Delhi's the worst."

"That's right. We're Bombay girls."

It made Al smile. "That's right."

"It's strange being with you in this room. It's strange thinking that this room looks unfamiliar to you."

"What does it look like to you?"

"This is where my grandparents used to live. There used to be a swing over there. And a Murphy bed. We came here every summer when I was a kid. I wish I knew what it felt like to see it for the first time."

"Why?"

"I can't imagine it, I guess. But I wonder if it scares you."

"Not feeling familiar? Of course not, why would it?"

"Nothing scares you."

"That's not true."

"You have bigger muscles than me."

"But smaller boobs."

"So what. I like them."

Al turned in her arms and brought her face close. Tejas put her fingers on the ridges of her spine, which she could feel through her T-shirt, and made Al seem like a creature, a stranger. Al's skin bruised and burned very easily, but Tejas' was thick and tough and spread the heat of the sun to her blood and muscles. She wondered so often what it would be like to be in Al's skin, in her body, to use her muscular arms, to look down at her small, sweet breasts. This lack of imagination made her feel so far away from Al. To look at a white leg in the shower going red with the heat of the water and think: me, my leg. What did India look like to Al? What did Tejas look like? She wanted to see, and couldn't, and never would.

"Do you ever think of telling your family here?"

"About what?"

"About me."

"No, never. What's the use? They wouldn't understand."

"You just act so different around them."

"Everybody does around family, don't they?"

"I guess so."

"You never told your grandma."

"She's almost dead," said Al. "It would just confuse her. You know that."

"Yes," Tejas said. She rested her hand against Al's left breast, where her heart thudded, feeling the vibration like her own. Al's parents were professors, and had happily introduced Tejas as their daughter's partner to the extended family at Thanksgiving before Al's Nana arrived. Tejas' dad had required a little more explaining, but he put up no protest, and played chess with Al after dinner while Tejas washed up. Their game was quiet but very long, and Tejas lay in bed listening to the shimmering the crickets made out of the summer night, imagining the click of the pieces moving across the board. The game was close, but she won, Al reported as she crawled into bed. Next to Al, Tejas could close her eyes and forget where she was, if only for a moment. But there was the rubbery smell of the Indian mattress and camphor from the sheets. Al's smell, the smell of her breath, the fennel seeds she had chewed after dinner. And then, sleep.

Eight of them went out to dinner: the groom-to-be, Tejas' cousin V; his mother; the aunt and uncle who were hosting Tejas and Al; two more cousins. Greetings were awkward—who to hug, who to shake hands with, whose feet to touch. She pushed Al out in front of her and made her say the phrase of practiced Hindi. Then it seemed easier. The mother of the groom clucked affectionately, and patted Al's cheek. The cousins smiled, shyly, at Al, who had dressed in a rush and still had wet hair. Tejas too, and her hands went up to her short hair uncertainly. They walked to a restaurant just across the street, still it took them a while to find a gap in the traffic. The aunts took the longest. Tejas sat next to V at dinner, and quickly ran out of things to ask him. Work was good. He was tired. His fiancée was smart and worked for a phone company, she was shy—they'd meet her tomorrow, at the wedding. How was life in America? Trying to put words to it seemed futile. She lived with and fucked a woman, spent weekends in parks and libraries, reading novels, she worked at an advocacy group for homeless youth, she drank beer on weeknights and went dancing. She told him things were good, they were fine. Her father was fine, sorry he couldn't make it. Her work was fine.

Across the table from her, Al was receiving an impromptu Hindi lesson from the uncle, which consisted of saying short phrases to her in a loud voice, and grinning at her response. Al soldiered through the meal with a kind of determined calm, finishing everything on her plate like Tejas instructed so as not to be rude. Yes, she liked the food, spicy food, though it made her nose run, and her face redden, yes, she liked India, she thought it was beautiful, she accepted their compliments on her own beauty and sweetness with a deepening blush, redder still than her sunburn. Then the conversation switched to Gujarati and Tejas tuned out. She studied V, his gentle hands that looked so much like her mother's. He had a round face pearled with sweat, and a satisfied smile. The food took her right to the limit of how much spice she could manage, it embarrassed her to struggle so much. She wiped her face.

"Next, your turn!" said an aunt to Tejas, suddenly in English. "When you get married?"

"Not soon," said Tejas, glancing over at her two unmarried cousins. But they were younger, and boys, so it could be years before they'd take the pressure off.

"Must be soon," said her uncle. "It's time for you."

"We find you a husband," said the other aunt.

"No," said Tejas. Her ears burned. "I don't need help."

"You need help, beti! Look at your hair. Who cut your hair off like that? Like a boy." The aunt, the groom's mother, clucked her tongue. She was round, the more talkative of the two, with smooth, fine, infinitely soft-looking skin, plump with age. "You tell her, Halberta."

"I think your hair looks lovely," said Al.

"No, no," said the aunt. "You tell her!"

"Maybe you should think about getting married," said Al. She looked amused. Her hair had dried with the thick evening air in no time. She looked tan and easy.

"Hanh," said the aunt, satisfied. "You see what I mean?"

They slept deeply that night, tired from the day's walking and the attention that listening to relatives requires, though once, in the middle of the night, Tejas woke disoriented, and blundered into Al's soft body as she got up to use the bathroom. Al's mouth opened, she let out a small sound. "Al?" said Tejas, now awake.

"Mmm?"

Tejas kissed her warm face. Al reached for her. It was like home. They kissed, mouths closed, Tejas climbed on top. Al's eyes came open, gray-blue in the thin light. Her face on the pillow was immensely large, soft with sweat and sleep. The more Tejas looked at her face, the larger and less familiar it seemed, like a word said over and over again until it loses meaning. Then it was just one thing next to another, the gentle curve of a nose, all shadow, the pits of shadows where eyes go, wet and reflective, blue cheeks, an open mouth. Tejas put a hand on Al's lips. Her breath huffed out of her, and warmed the fingers. They moved against each other, being quiet. Tejas closed her eyes. They had been holding tense and apart for weeks, it felt sweet to let night touch everything with forgetting. Then

Tejas began to forget everything. Her closed eyes colored everything black, as though she were in a pit with herself, or submerged in warm ocean, swimming against it, and tightening, feeling herself rise and build. She was building herself, out of nothing, it felt urgent. Her eyes came open. The body was the plainest truth, it was everything. What was her own name? The core came alive. Alberta, Alberta.

The wedding was noisy; they danced in the procession together in front of the horse. Al was clapping, laughing, sweating, in a gold sari and jewels in her hair, hands stained with fresh henna. Everything about her seemed pale and out of place, and Tejas, tugging at her own sari, leaf green and endlessly sequined, felt a strange, leaping feeling start at the pit of her, and move upward. There were drums, a trumpet, the music was thick and overpowering as they moved through the narrow street, pressed on both sides by buildings lined in every place by centuries of dirt, still beautiful, almost trembling with the noise and crowd. The family loved to see Al dance; she took it up gamely, laughing with them. It was too loud to speak. They arrived at the hall, and the bride was there, shining from every part of her, glittering even at the fingernails. Her cheeks were pale and fawny, her lips carefully made, red. Someone anointed V's face with sandalwood paste. Pictures, pictures, pictures, then the groom went with the family into the hall to await the official arrival of his bride. He sat on the decorated seat in front of the fire and checked his phone.

Al and Tejas watched the bride carried in, sitting in a covered palanquin, red and spangled, carried in on the backs of her cousins and brothers. The drum felt like a shared heartbeat, racing with the excitement of the moment she would step out, eyes lowered, and be looked at by all the eyes, shining for them like a divine thing. She looked so calm, downcast, radiant, her shyness, it felt as though they should ask for her blessing. This would never be hers—Tejas's—none of it. To have family come and carry you on their backs to the next place. For a moment it made her want to cry: she had not chosen it. And as the ceremony dragged, the monotonous Sanskrit, the thousand flowered offerings, Tejas let her eyes fall upon the bride, again and again. Now V dabbed at his brow with a handkerchief, now touched hands with the bride over an offering, saying a phrase in his mouth and then giving it to her to say. All around them the guests were gossiping, and greeting one another, and laughing, the children raced around the hall, screaming, ignored. The heat from the day mixed with the heat from the fire and the smoke.

Al shifted in her seat. She wiped at her eye, there was something in it. Then she took up Tejas's hand and kissed it, quick, when nobody was looking.

THE NEIGHBORS

A T THAT TIME my daughter was eight, and my son had just been born. I sat on the front lawn with him and stopped him from putting fists of grass into his mouth. It was late July, and hot, a rich, thick heat that reminded me of the descent into summers of my childhood in India. My son gazed up at the trees in wonder. Still small enough to look slightly absurd, almost like a fish with the gaping mouth and eyes, but then he would move his head a little bit, wave his arms, and he would look suddenly, startlingly human.

My daughter came running down the street with no shoes on. Only this morning I had combed her hair, but you wouldn't know it to look at her.

"Mom, someone's moving in to Mrs. Hildebrandt's house."

There was a moving truck pulled up in the driveway of the empty house at the end of the street. We could see them through the trees. A girl—then two—emerged from the passenger's side of the cab, from the driver's a tall man, then a short-haired woman.

"Where are your shoes?" I said. I watched the family as they opened the door to their new house. In fact I had been keeping an eye on the place since it became vacant. It had a similar floor plan to ours, all the houses on the street were Eichlers, but better sun in the yard, and the last owner, an elderly woman who had died some months ago, planted roses that bloomed even in her absence, and not one but two fruit trees, lemon and orange. The girls ran in first. The woman stood a few paces away from the door, and the man behind her. She turned to the man to say something to him. She was much smaller than him, and had to lean up to do it. The man put his hand on her head, right at the nape of her neck. She looked so vulnerable there, at the back of the head, with her hair so short, short like a baby's, so close to the soft skull. His hand there was familiar to me, the gesture full of the brutal tenderness of husbands. I couldn't see her face to tell if she was happy or sad.

That evening I lay my son down in his crib and went to the bathroom to comb my hair. Almost as soon as I put him down he began to cry, and the door didn't blunt the noise. I wanted to comb my hair. When I was younger, my hair was thick and rich and scented, after washing I used to spread it on a wicker basket under which burned a lump of frangipani. Once as a girl, finishing the thread I was using to sew a dress for my home crafts class, I had plucked a strand of my own hair and threaded the needle with it. It was long enough and it held.

Of course I lost quite a bit of my hair after my two pregnancies, which my gynecologist told me is common. For a while I thought my hair would grow back, but it never did. Then I began to comb it less frequently, sometimes I forgot for days. I had remembered today because of the woman and her short hair, which had shocked me. But she had seemed beautiful, even from such a distance. I could hear the mewling cries of my son, rising in pitch and frequency. The reflection in the mirror surprised me. Who was that woman? I thought of myself as young, a girl, and hardly ever looked at myself anymore. Then I began to comb my hair, tugging hard at the snarls, so hard that my scalp bled. When I was finished it lay flat and shining against my skull.

It was three days later when I opened the door to the neighbor woman. She had baked a batch of pale cookies and seemed to be visiting the entire neighborhood with them. Up close she was older than I expected, older than me, her face all angles, as well as her body, which was so slender it was boney. She wore a pale blue dress that left her legs and freckled arms bare. Under the right eye the skin was slightly darkened, the ghost of a bruise. Her two girls stood behind her. The elder was surely my daughter's age, the younger, no more than three, plump, with bright gold hair, like a little doll.

"God it's hot as anything out here," the woman said, handing me the cookies. A bit of hair stuck to her damp forehead. "I didn't feel like baking, but when you move you should always bake something for the neighbors, I think. Anyway, I hope you're not allergic to anything or vegan, they're lemon cookies—lemons from the tree—" she pointed to her yard, "I didn't want them to go to waste. I'm making marmalade with the rest of them—the oranges are too sour to eat. I don't know anything about orange trees."

The sound of the sprinkler, two houses down, hissed up between us. The woman smelled of flowers, yellow flowers I imagined. Other neighbors had made similar overtures over the years. But after a little while, they left me alone. "I don't know anything either about orange trees," I said.

"I'm sorry, I didn't even say my name," she said. She was older than me, but her face looked young, and flushed slightly like a girl's. "I'm Luisa. And this is Camille and Geenie. My husband, Richard, is at work. We moved in to the house down the street. They're shy, the girls are. Say hi, girls."

"Hi," they said. The elder's voice sounded bored, the younger's was a whisper.

"Would you like to come in?" I said. "My husband is also at work."

Luisa looked down at her two girls, then looked back at me. A strand of gold, terminating in a tiny star, hung from each ear. "That would be wonderful."

I led them inside—seeing the shoes at the door, they took theirs off on instinct—and sat them down in the living room, where the baby, in his swing, had began to bunch up his face, but he relaxed when he saw me, held out his arms. I carried him so much in those days that my body had gotten used to the extra weight. When I put him down, there was a feeling that came over me, almost like vertigo, a mixture of dizziness and exhilaration, of terrible, terrific lightness. It wasn't like this with my daughter, who was always independent and self-contained as a cat, and who had learned to read when she was five, which was when I lost her to her mind's vast interior. She was her father's child.

"A baby!" said Luisa, "He's beautiful. How old is he?"

"Four months," I said. He smelled of milk, my baby, and he grasped my shirt in his hands and wiped his nose against my shoulder. "His name is Manoj. I'll get my daughter, I think she's your age, Geenie."

Then I went to the bottom of the stairs and called her, sweetly and urgently, so they would think I was a good mother. "Manisha!"

She took a while to appear. Backlit by the window at the top of the stairs, there was a crown of hair frizzed around her head, and I couldn't see her eyes. The soles of her feet were also out of my vision, but their state I could guess; black from her barefoot summer, black and leathery, like the child of a beggar. "What."

I spoke to her in Hindi. "The neighbors are downstairs. The new neighbors. Will you come down?"

Her body held the heaviness of a sleepwalker, but she

came, and followed me back into the living room. Luisa sat on the sofa with a girl on either side of her, and they were talking in low voices. I could hear the unmistakable sound of whining, and the equally unmistakable sound of stern hushing. "Manisha?" said Luisa, she said it like an Indian, with a soft uh sound instead of a hard a Americans put in the first syllable. *Man*isha, my daughter came home crying with anger her first day at school from the cruel mispronunciation. "This is Geenie, and Camille, and I'm Luisa. Geenie's going to be starting fifth grade in the fall."

"Manisha too," I said. Geenie was a year older, then: Manisha had skipped a grade. She had been a misfit before the change, and she was a misfit now, because of her age, and, I suspected, her solitariness, which came off as cool pride. "Manisha, do you want to show Geenie your room?"

Manisha looked at me, not a little warily. The mention of school had shaken her out of something, the thick dreaminess I had seen on her at breakfast.

"You can show her all your books," I said.

"Okay," she said. I could see her eying Geenie, her pretty clothes, the little ribboned clips in her hair. Their feet were quiet on the stairs, carpeted to cushion a child's fall, dark to hide stains. I shifted the baby in my arms. He was sucking his heel, then his fist.

"Can I hold the baby?" Camille whispered to her mother.

"Babies aren't dolls, Cami, they're not toys."

"I know," she said. Her eyes were caught on my son's. Hers were pale blue, like her mother's dress. "Can I?"

It was all addressed to her mother, but I said, "Go wash your hands, the bathroom is just right over there. Then you can hold him."

We watched her pad out of the room.

"You have a beautiful house," said Luisa. The sink turned on. Camille was on her tiptoes, we could see her through the open door.

"Same as yours," I said.

"No, I mean, the way you've arranged it. The furniture is so beautiful. It's very bright and friendly. You have a good eye for things—you and your husband, I should say."

Of course, it had all been me, and I smiled with pleasure. It wasn't often I had guests, though I did my best to keep the house clean. "Come, let's have some of these cookies."

"No, no. I've had enough already," she said. "You have them later."

"Where did you move from?"

"Colorado—Denver. Richard had a job there."

"What does he do?"

"He's in sales. And I'm an artist."

"An artist?"

"Yes. I paint. Mostly watercolor."

"What do you paint?"

"Oh, lots of things, really. I paint those two a lot, if they sit still. We lived in Arizona before Denver, and I liked living in the desert. I liked painting how dry and red everything was out there, especially in the evenings. Richard calls it my Georgia O'Keeffe period, of course."

"How do you have the time for it?"

"It's just a matter of practice." She had slipped her legs beside her on the couch. There was something avian about her, the elegance and ease of her pose. Yet I felt something unsettled in her too.

"But the space I mean."

"The space?" she said. "Usually we make some space in the garage."

"Not that kind of space," I said, but I didn't know how to say what I meant, and let it drop. A small silence followed.

"And you, what do you do?"

"When I was young I wanted to be a pilot," I said.

The sink switched off. Camille's little hands were red.

"Come here," I said. She sat next to me on the love seat. She smelled of my soap—sandalwood— and kid's sweat, and thinly, the floral scent of her mother. Sitting with her back against the back of the love seat, her feet just reached the end of the cushion. "If he cries you mustn't be upset, okay? He's shy, just like you."

I eased Manoj into her arms. "Keep the head up, like this."

I could see the storm gathering in his face. I held his hand, and sang to him the Indian anthem, which always soothed him. He began to laugh.

Late at night, I was awoken by the sound of glass breaking, or glass broke in my dream, and I awoke. I was flung awake. My husband lay on his back, sleeping, and the baby was asleep too, in his crib, which we kept in our room. Father and son slept dead like each other, bodies gone thick and heavy and soft, slept without moving, barely breathing until they woke. My son's sleep was particularly disconcerting, because he slept with his eyes half open, and during the weeks after he was born I had often held a mirror under his nose, to see if it fogged up with his breath. I went to my daughter's room, and stood in the doorway, casting my shadow over the floor. The room had filled up with her breathing, warm and not wholly pleasant. She curled on her bed with all the blankets flung off dramatically. Her window looked onto the street, from the vantage of the second story. I stood there in my nightgown. The lawn below me was nearly blue in moonlight and streetlight. There was someone in the street. I saw him, his shoulders, his hot blonde hair, then lifted my gaze, to where all the lights were on in the house down the street. I must have stood there for a long time. I felt my own mind, tingling like a limb come awake. The street was empty, then the light went off in the house, still I stood, remembering a night long ago, when I stood at a window in another country. It wasn't nostalgia. My life was crowded then with family, and I worked hard. Yet this space was there. I thought about it for a long time. I couldn't say whether I was happy, or sad, or sorry for myself.

Then my daughter cried out in her sleep, and just like that, the space closed. My mind and body turned to her. She blinked up at me, like she had as a baby, with her black eyes. "Mom?"

Was she awake or dreaming? I felt irritation and tenderness in equal parts. "Go back to sleep," I said.

"I was being eaten, someone was eating me," she said.

"Just a dream," I said. She was scared, shaking and I held her, she allowed me.

"You don't want me anymore," she said.

"What?"

"You don't want me anymore."

"You're dreaming," I said. "You'll feel embarrassed about this in the morning."

Every morning, I combed my daughter's hair before I fed both the children breakfast. It was a challenge, because the baby was always clingy right after he woke up and my daughter had trouble sitting still for more than a few minutes at a time. If I put the baby down, he would begin to cry, and Manisha would use the distraction to run off. Then I would have to start the whole process over.

"You said Manisha means mind. You said that the mind is the most important. That's what you said."

"Mind is important, hair is important. Already you run around the neighborhood like a wild thing."

"So my hair is as important as my mind?"

"No." I had put the baby in a sling against my chest, so my hands were free. The sling reminded me of the peasant women in the fields, who worked for hours with their babies tied to their bodies in old saris. But mine I bought at Target. "It is important to look nice for people."

"Why?"

"I don't know why. I don't know why you are so difficult, why you don't just listen to me."

"Because you don't make sense!"

July mornings were cool and felt strange on the skin after waking; afterward the days became brutally hot. The baby was still small enough to bathe in the sink, and I bathed him often and massaged his body with oil. Manisha came in only when she got hungry, and I cleaned the house and made sure the dishes were out of the dishwasher, made lists of things I needed to get from the store, paid all the bills and called the health insurance company about a birth-related expense they had not yet reimbursed. I was in the process of applying for citizenship, which also produced a large amount of paperwork. I fed the baby, changed the baby, put the baby to sleep and picked him back up when he woke, sang to the baby, talked to the baby, read to him.

Manisha came in and reported that Luisa was letting her kids run through the sprinklers. "Geenie has a bikini!"

"You don't want a bikini."

"Yes, I do."

I sighed. "Wasn't it you who was only caring about the mind this morning?"

She shrugged.

"Do you want to go and run out in the sprinklers with them?"

"I don't know."

"We could put the sprinklers on here."

"Then we'll be copying them."

"Fine."

Luisa was stretched out on a plastic lawn chair in shorts and a tank top and a hat that covered her face. She was reading a gigantic magazine. She waved when she saw us approaching.

"Glad you're back, Manisha. Brought your suit?"

Manisha pulled up her T-shirt, showing the swimsuit underneath.

"Go on then."

Manisha hesitated. Geenie and Camille had not taken any notice of her. They looked half-wild on the lawn. They would grow up to be beautiful, like their mother, with their small faces, Geenie's heart-shaped, and Camille's oval, their wide eyes and little noses and soft, elegant mouths. Their beauty was startling because they were so unaware of it; it was strange to see them act with such abandon, like children, with those faces. Like two princesses from a storybook I read Manisha, one dark, one fair, the water glittering on their skin. As the sprinkler changed direction, it fanned into a rainbow. Manisha took off her shirt and shorts and stood barefoot in her yellow bathing suit. Her belly puffed out, and the way she stood with her feet turned outward made her look like a duck.

"Girls, Manisha's here," said Luisa. The girls looked up from their play. Camille's knees were stained with mud. Her little pink tongue came out of her mouth and licked her cheek. "We're playing cats."

"No we're not," said Geenie. She was, as reported, wearing a ruffled pink two-piece, the top of which lay flat against her chest. She cast a scornful look at her sister. "Cats hate water."

"Not all do," said Camille.

"Yeah, all do. They're from the desert."

"I like cats," I heard Manisha say. She was allergic, and had an instinctual fear reaction to most animals, throwing her hands up to protect her face when they came near.

"We're going to get one, Mom says," offered Camille.

"We'll see," said Luisa.

The baby and I were both sweating, but I was glad at least that I wasn't pregnant in this heat. "It's hard enough being responsible for the two of you. Though at this point maybe a third life wouldn't make any difference." She had put down her magazine, and she took her hat off to fan herself. On the underside of her arm there was a constellation of yellow marks. "Tell me, how long have you lived in the neighborhood?"

"Well, let's see. Manisha was four and a half when we moved. So I would say about three and a half years."

"I hope we stay here that long."

"How long were you in Denver?"

"Only a few months. Richard's job. Three schools in two years."

"That must be hard on them."

"But you know, I moved around a lot as a kid, my dad was in the army—so I think of myself as sort of a gypsy now. Richard says I romanticize my childhood, but he wasn't there, was he? I like change, moving around."

The baby sneezed. It was a tiny noise, but it rocked him. He looked up at me, bewildered, and I stroked his cheek so he would feel reassured. Ever so slightly, I shifted him in my arms, so that the bruises at my throat would be visible between my dupatta and the neck of my blouse. I looked to see if Luisa noticed; if she had her face didn't register it.

"Moving around so much—it must be nice, in some ways."

"Yes, it is."

"To feel . . . how does it feel?"

"Just about how you'd expect, I think. Sometimes it's hard, you get so attached to a place. There are so many places to miss. And you just have to pack everything up, your clothes and pots and things, you start to hate your stuff. You want to throw it all away and start over on the other end."

I remembered how I felt when I was young, slight as a plastic bag, caught on nothing, riding the wind. But I had been caught. Again, I shifted the baby in my arms, more clumsily, less carefully, to show her where, three days ago, hands had squeezed my neck as though pulping a fruit. I stood there with her in an expectant silence, feeling the start of a sweeping relief, like a person in a wreck who sees through the windshield the Jaws of Life. I had, until this moment, never said it to anyone, not even to myself. Instead I had extinguished each event at the root of the candle, before it had time in my mind to burn. Then I looked at her and realized she was refusing. Not only to say it, but to see, just to see it, to see me. Her eyes were hard and faraway, the eyes of a stranger—which, of course, she was. With haste I covered the spots on my neck and looked away.

There was a cry from the girls, and I turned around to see Manisha tripped or fallen in the grass. She was wet now, and lay for a minute stunned on the ground, face-down. Geenie and Camille stood still, grazed every now and then by the edge of the sprinkler, Geenie's face proud, Camille's full of the innocence I hoped she would always have, would never leave her.

"She tripped," said Geenie.

"Are you okay, Manisha?" said Luisa. She rose from her lawn chair but didn't approach my daughter. Manisha lifted her wet face. There was grass stuck in her hair. For a moment I could not bear to look at her face, full of humiliated anger. She looked too much like me.

"Manisha?" I said.

She would not cry. She came to her hands and knees, then picked herself up gingerly, and, as though her legs were untrustworthy, treaded carefully over the wet lawn. When she had reached the sidewalk, she began to run.

"Manisha!" I called. She didn't turn around. I watched the black soles of my daughter's feet slapping the pavement.

A SIMPLE COMPOSITION

WHEN I WAS sixteen my parents decided I should take up the sitar, and I began to receive lessons from a great musician who had fallen on lean times. I had little talent, and he was a strict teacher. He often yelled me to tears. "These are the fingers of a princess," he would say, examining my hand for calluses and dropping it with scorn. My palm felt hot as I brought it back into my lap. "Again," and as I began to play he would take up his instrument in a fit of irritated passion and override me with his music. "Like this." He had thick brows and a fat, jolly nose that seemed out of character with the rest of his features; he always appeared to be scowling. As he played the sitar his face became no more beautiful, but it was touched by the grace of the music. His sharp eyes closed and his fingers moved with a subtlety I could never hope for. A simple composition, like the one he chose for me, became something else in the belly of his sitar, something distilled to its essence. It was longing for god, or the longing for perfection. The longing for childhood or mother, the longing for lost days, or for a lover. His notes were never singular; he bent them into each other, playing just as time passes, one moment blending into the next. When he finished I could see tears in his eyes.

After a while I started to practice for hours in the evenings, and my fingertips toughened. I began to love the sitar like I would a living thing, feeling tenderness as she lay in my arms, with my fingers moving up and down her slender neck. But I could feel my lack of talent as my skill grew. Even to my own ears the music I produced sounded flat and rigid. I could bend the notes and quiver them, but the animating spirit that was supposed to be there underneath never appeared; it was like manipulating a puppet. But I felt it, that ache. Perhaps this is why I fell in love.

The lessons took place in the sitting room of my house, where my mother sewed clothes for the poor while my teacher scolded me. It was dark in the sitting room—the curtains were always drawn to protect the furniture—and stuffy, with just the overhead ceiling fan that turned too slowly to do more than stir the hot air and often went off altogether with the power cuts. I had been left alone with my teacher only three times: when the cook had needed special instruction on the night's meal, when the leather-sole repairman returned with our shoes, and when my youngest brother had fallen from his bicycle and came crying home with a scraped knee. During the first two instances I was tense, but my sitar teacher hardly seemed to notice any change. During the third, he told me, "You're improving."

"Not much."

"True. I can still see the work in your fingers."

"You have a gift so you can't imagine what it's like not to."

He looked at me sharply. He was not a young man. And I knew almost nothing about him, where he lived, if he was married. Yet in that look, some knowledge passed to me, innocent as I was, about how he was thinking of me. He was considering me the way men consider women, with a grudging appreciation, even deference to their beauty. I could feel myself grow hot, not just my face but my entire body, alone in that close room with him.

"You give yourself an excuse that way. You're too easily distracted."

I can remember being sixteen and feeling that love heavy in my chest. I was shy, and had a quiet face and neat black hair, and I was so dark that my marriage prospects would have been grim had my parents not been well-off. At school the girls thought I was dull and ignored me. At home, I had three brothers, all younger, who filled the house with noise, while I, even with my music, occupied the rooms very quietly, taking up very little space and demanding no attention. But attention mattered little to me, and less now that my desire for it was concentrated to a single source.

When the afternoons became hotter my mother dozed in her chair during my lessons. There was a growing awareness between us, my sitar teacher and I. He began to scold me even more fiercely for my ineptitude. But I started to realize that his sharp words were a substitute for something else, and I did not cry. In fact, it was all I could do to keep from smiling. One day, he asked if I could meet him at a park that evening. Not so much asked as told me, quietly but with no sense of wrongdoing as my mother slept. The park was on the other side of the city, one I had not been to before. I didn't think my mother would let me go, and in the intervening hours I became more and more agitated trying to think of an excuse. Ultimately, it was simple: I told her I was meeting a schoolmate to study. Since the days were long in summer I would likely be home before dark. She took no notice of the wild look my eyes had. I bathed and put flowers in my hair and wrapped myself carefully in a fresh milk-blue sari. My hands were shaking from excitement as I paid the rickshaw wallah.

My sitar teacher was waiting for me by the entrance. He had not changed out of the clothes I had seen him in last, and was soaked through by his own sweat. He was smoking a beedi, and when he saw me he stubbed it out carefully and put it in his pocket. His face looked rough and unshaven. He asked immediately if I was skipping my evening practice in order to meet with him. I told him I would practice when I got home. We began to walk in the park. It was lush, full of flowers and green trees, but it seemed oddly empty, especially for this time of day. The evening light was becoming a heavy orange, almost metallic. As we moved through the park I realized it was not empty: there were lovers hidden in every corner, behind bushes and low walls, and leaning against the pillars of the crumbling ornamental buildings. Yet he didn't touch me. He told me that he was four years old when he picked up the sitar for the first time: his father's. His arms were just wide enough to span the instrument, yet after he managed an awkward hold on it music came to him effortlessly and pierced him with joy. It was the joy, he said, of a loved one returned to you—one thought dead, lost forever. He knew he had only to wait for the skill of his body to catch up to the music inside him.

Nothing felt like that to me. I didn't want to tell him so. To me, music was the unity and division of tones, like a painting was the arrangement of colors. Beauty was a mathematical certainty that arose from a precisely correct combination. It was impossible for me to imagine him as a boy.

"You didn't tell your mother where you were going?"

"No."

He nodded. I studied him, his curls, his slender, beautiful fingers encased by rings, which he would take off with a kind of ceremony as he settled down for each lesson. His gaze was directed straight ahead of him, yet I knew that he was aware of me by just how he seemed to ignore my presence. Somewhere in the distance, there was an odd sound, like a rusty gate opening.

"What is that?"

"A peacock," he said.

"No, is it?" I said. I knew the mewling cry of peacocks.

"There's something wrong with him."

The noise sounded again. It was less metallic than the last. There was something animal, ragged in it. Then the peacock came into view, brilliant and absurd. He had a strange, almost drunken gait, and when he got closer we saw knots of pink flesh where his eyes should have been. He heard our footsteps scuffing in the dust, and began to panic, running a wide, wavering arc through the dust of the path.

"What's happened to him?"

"Someone's cut out his eyes."

"You think a person did it?"

"Not a peacock."

"Why would anyone do that?"

He shook his head. "Poor fellow."

We walked for some time and it began to grow dark. The evening had swollen around me, I had sweated through my blouse. I feared I was utterly ordinary. The air smelled thickly of flowers, and in my desperation it became a cloying smell, smothering, and I wanted to pull the jasmine from my hair and throw it on the ground. He took me suddenly by the arm and led me behind a low wall where ten or twenty feet away two people moved against each other in the growing dimness. They made no noise, but I could see them: an unbuttoned blouse, hands that gripped tightly to the naked flesh. The sky was low, pinking. My sitar teacher kissed me and put his hands on my breasts.

His mouth tasted like the beedi he had been smoking, and some other, sweet-bitter thing—alcohol, I realized later. This should have been the moment of my truest joy, the kind of joy he had described as a young child first picking up the sitar. But it felt like nothing, worse than nothing. I did not expect pain—but what had I expected? I started to feel for my voice, at first curiously, then frantically, as he pulled at the fabric of my sari and pressed his flesh into mine. At first I couldn't find it. Then it was there, small but there, like a little white moth. I felt it come up in my mouth as he moved against me. I swallowed it down.

So I was not a virgin when I married Hritish, though I led him to believe differently. On our wedding night we fell asleep in the petaled bed as soon as we removed our elaborate clothes, consummating our marriage four days later, shyly, and with genuine ineptitude during the afternoon. Whatever I had worried about disappeared when I saw his bashfulness and inexperience. It made me gentle toward him, holding him in that act of love no differently than a mother holding her boy; it is pity, I thought, the way a mother holds her boy. In the morning I woke before him and watched him sleep, this half-stranger, who had grown up in my neighborhood, and whom I had passed by sometimes walking to or from school. Love had not come yet, though they told me it would, growing slowly over the years of our lives together. What I felt was a kind of detached fondness, which often I drew out of me to hold up and inspect like an X-ray, looking for signs of growth or change. Once, when he placed a sweet in my mouth, I thought I observed a change, a new tender shoot. He took my braid in his hand and wrapped it around his fist, marveling at its strength. And wept during our first true fight, tears that startled, even frightened me, as his eyes got so red. I touched his hair, saying, "A husband shouldn't cry." And then after a while he stopped.

"Will you play something for me?"

But I would not touch my sitar. Sometimes when my husband was at work I walked by the home of my sitar teacher. He lived in a small bungalow behind a wall that was topped with shards of glass; through the gate I could see a garden, and I could hear children's voices coming from the other side of the gate. Once I saw a woman going through, a young woman with flowers in her hair. After that I stopped walking there. Each day that summer, the heat that collected in the small rooms of our flat was intolerable, and we brought our mattresses up to the roof and slept without blankets. Then my husband received a scholarship and we went to Germany. The air in Mainz was thin and dry, not like the heat of home. It was lighter and deadlier, this fall air. My husband went to school at the university, studying particle physics, and I spent my days in the apartment they rented to students, which, though it was not much larger than our flat at home, seemed set up for a kind of life I didn't know how to live yet. I had thought that I would feel like a new person when I came to Germany. It was not that I was lonely, no lonelier than I had ever been. But I had some difficulty sleeping. I missed those nights on the roof, lying on a thin cotton mattress. I missed the looseness of those nights, watching the stuck kites in the trees shifting as a breeze came through, the fat orange moon.

We went one evening to the house of my husband's advisor, who was Gujarati, and his German wife. This professor had been living in Germany for so long that he now ate meat, and there was no food for us at the dinner because even the salad had bacon. I didn't know whether it was less polite to keep some food on my plate and not eat it, or to not put any food on my plate at all. I was afraid to look at Hritesh because I was sure that whatever he was doing was the wrong thing, and he would be doing it with a smile at the center of his burning face. I was hungry, and watched the professor and his wife eat. The professor's dark face had taken on a German look, a frowning, inward expression.

"You don't like German food?" said the wife, finally, as I sat in front of my empty plate.

"We are vegetarians," I said.

"It's only chicken," she said. Her arms were white and bare and looked soft, but she was plain and wore a shapeless blouse. "Here."

I covered my plate with my hands. The professor looked at me with a smile on his face—what could have been called a smile. Some time later he said a phrase to me in German, but I didn't know he was speaking to me, and kept my eyes fixed politely away. He said it again. This time my husband said, "He's asking you how your German is coming."

I said the one phrase I knew in German, "Ich spreche kein Deutsch."

The professor replied in English. "Smart man, your husband. He's picking it up."

"You like this city, Mainz?" said the wife.

"I haven't seen much of it," I said.

"Sie hat immer Angst," he said to Hritesh. "Do you tell her about your research?"

"I don't want to bore her."

"You don't bore me." And I noticed, now, that he had grown thin, my husband. His face, especially, was thin, and had a restless quality to it. His eyes were unusually bright. After dinner, we walked home in the cold, what felt like bitter cold to me, though it was not yet winter. At this time of night, the city was lit yellow, spilling over with students, laughing and arguing in their harsh, orderly language. "Why didn't you tell them that we were vegetarians?"

"I thought he knew."

"Is he a good man, this professor of yours?"

"I think so. He's brilliant."

"What did he say about me in German?"

"He said you were scared."

"Scared? Scared of what?"

But he didn't know. "We'll have to have them over for dinner," he said, with a kind of despair.

My husband glanced often out the window when we were at home. He had acquired habits I found odd. First thing when he arrived, he ran his finger under the rims of the three lampshades in our apartment, and sometimes he took the framed picture of his father off the wall and removed the back. Then he would replace it and clean the glass, almost apologetically, freshly anointing his father's fore-head with kumkum and sandalwood paste, as we did to honor our dead.

"What are you looking for?"

"No—nothing. It comforts me."

He did seem comforted by his actions: they eased him. After dinner we would watch the one channel on TV that sometimes showed English movies. When I was alone, I began to go on long walks. I wanted to get my skin used to or even immune to the cold. I wanted my body to accept Germany, its new home. It was true, I had spent so much time in the flat because I was scared to leave it. I was constantly worried I was going to be made a fool. And as the days grew colder and shorter, the flat seemed to grow smaller and closer, contracting around me like a fist. I walked around the university, which was hundreds of years old, and decorated with the statues of serious-nosed men. But for all my worry, hardly anyone seemed to notice me. I bought coffee at the cafeteria and drank it slowly as I sat. This is the future, I thought, I had wondered so much about. It was here now. I could stop wondering what would happen to me.

"Anuradha?" When I looked up, it was my husband's

professor, carrying his food on a tray. An odd hour to eat, not a mealtime at all, nearing four.

"Where is Hritish?"

He shrugged. "You imagine he is always with me. Were you meeting him?"

"No." Then I said, "You eat here?"

"Yes, on occasion. It's not bad."

"Your wife doesn't make?"

"No, she's not a good wife like you, packing lunches. I'm going to eat this in my office if you'd like to join me."

His office was in a squat, modern building that looked out on the river. It was warm in the room, and he sweated as he ate, wiping at his forehead with a napkin. Again I watched him eat. He had thick, sensual lips and intelligent eyes, tar-colored and cutting. But there had once been a softness I could make out in his face, in his eyes. I thought I could see the kind of boy he had been, brash and loved, and happy. When he was finished, he belched into his closed fist.

"Your husband is transferring out of my department."

"What?"

"He's going to mathematics. Or trying, at any rate."

"He didn't say anything about it."

"Your husband," he said, shaking his head. "Your husband is coming up with some strange ideas."

He placed his tray on the stack of trays he had accumulated in his office. The books on the shelves were not just science—I spotted three slim volumes of Urdu poetry.

"You speak Urdu?"

"Not anymore. I used to."

"I studied it in college."

"I've never read more beautiful poetry. I can't read those books anymore, but I remember what they were like. I've lost the language." There was something about the way he was looking at me. I had never felt physical desire before, and was not sure I felt it now. It was my heart coming up in my mouth. Beating loud in my ears, my heart.

"Are you happy here, in Germany?"

"Yes," I said, automatically. "Are you?"

He went to lock the door. Then he came to where I was sitting and leaned down to put his mouth on mine. I could taste the meat in his mouth from his sandwich. I stood up and pressed my body against him. I was on my period, but he said he did not mind. There was nothing in it, no shyness. There was no anger. It was deliberate and almost tender. At one point, realizing we would be visible to the students below, he went to turn off the light. Outside, the river was a flat sheet of silver, shining so hard it hurt to look at, even as the sky was dimming, the thick gray clouds seeming to absorb all that brilliance. Without giving anything back.

At home, I washed myself and made supper and waited past dark for my husband, who now kept irregular hours at the lab. I was not altered, my hair was still neat, my clothes and my face. It stunned me, my own neatness, my lack of change. I thought, this is not the woman I have become, this is the woman I have always been. When Hritesh finally arrived, I looked hard at him, wanting to feel pain. What a tired face my husband had for someone so young. His skin was a rich nut-brown but darker and delicate under his eyes. "You didn't tell me you were transferring departments."

"I didn't think you'd be interested."

"I saw Professorji at the cafeteria."

"Oh god," he said, "we still have to invite them, you remember? To dinner."

"Look at you. You're working too hard."

"I'm close," he said. "I'm close to something."

"Close to what?"

But he wouldn't—or couldn't—say. Later I found him standing worried at the window, looking out at the street.

"You see that van?"

I looked. There, parked across the street, was the white delivery van of the bakery around the corner.

"What is it?"

He stood there for a long while. Then he came away from the window. "Nothing."

The van was gone in the morning. As he was leaving for work he said, "Tell me if the van comes back."

"You want me to call you at the lab if the van comes back?"

"No, no, don't call. Just write down the time." Then, at the look on my face, he said, "Forget it. Forget it, *na*? Don't do anything."

But there was, quite suddenly, a miracle that was happening outside: it was snowing. I had seen snow in movies, but it was fake snow, only soapsuds, and looked different than this. Real snow was so small, and came all at once, but gently, and fell in a way I had never seen anything fall before, with none of the weight and force of rain, with profound and unhurried silence. We stood like children at the window. The snow touched everything we could see, like light. We were afraid only because we didn't know how it would feel in our fingers and our hair and on our faces. But after a while Hritish became brave and handed me my coat. Outside, there was a quality of silence I had never heard before, even in this quiet country. I caught a wafer of snow on my finger. I licked it. It was a pure drop of water, tasting of nothing, holy water. Hritish, I saw, was standing quite still, like I was, as the white gathered shaggy in his hair and eyebrows and eyelashes and on the shoulders of his coat. There was something absurd about the way he stood there, almost unblinking, but I was so glad. He had sensed, as I had, the sacredness of the living moment, the sacred quality of that silence, and become, like me, utterly still.

Yet we bore no resentment toward the children who broke into the quiet with their shrieks and their snowballs and their stamping feet. We went inside, shook the snow from our hair, and wiped our dripping faces. He was smiling, my husband, he had a good smile, the smile of a shy young girl. "You'll be late," I said.

"Anu—"

"You'll be late," I said, pushing him lightly toward the door. When he was gone, I sat down on the sofa. I thought I would cry. But I didn't cry. I just sat there.

For two weeks, I watched myself. I cooked the meals, as I always had, making the sad substitutions with German vegetables and spices that made my own cooking unfamiliar to me. The snow melted and the world became ordinary again, even drab, with all that mud. I walked around the university, but I didn't see the professor, except for once, talking to a student outside the physics building, and I quickly turned around and walked the other way before he saw me. My husband during this time pulled further and further into himself. I saw him once too, on campus, through the lighted window of a classroom where he sat in the last row, furiously writing notes. At home, he seemed almost apologetic, and talked to me gently, as if compensating for some hurt he had caused me. The matter of the van was not mentioned. Some days it sat parked for hours when he was at the university but left before he got home.

Then one evening the van had not gone when my husband got home, and he became agitated. He was frightened, I could see, and I began to feel frightened too. He kept walking to the window and looking out at the van. He wouldn't tell me what was the matter. He was suppressing tears: they trembled on the lids of his eyes and wet his eyelashes. I sat with him, talking to him quietly

in our mother tongue, which seemed to calm him just a
bit, to make his suffering just bearable. When I ran out of
things to say he begged me to keep speaking, so I recited
the poems I had learned in school, and then, when I came
to the end of those, nursery rhymes. I talked and talked for
what felt like hours, until my throat and tongue were tired,
even my jaw. Sometimes I would fall into a light doze, and
wake to see him in such a terrifying state of despair I would
rouse myself completely and begin talking again. Then it
was dawn. He was tired out. He stretched his body on
the bed and slept. I washed my face in the sink with cold
water, put on a clean sari, and went to the office of his
advisor. It was too early, and the building was locked; I
waited outside for some time. It was cold, and it was good
to feel cold. In my tiredness I leaned against it, pressed it
close to me to keep me awake. I felt love for my husband
all at once, bright as sunlight, breathtaking. I thought of
him on our wedding day, his smiling face surrounded by
red and white flowers. After a while a janitor came and
unlocked the door and I went to the third floor and sat
opposite the professor's office, and, in the warmth of the
hallway, dozed until he came and prodded me awake. We
went into his office. He was angry to see me and said that
it "looked bad" for me to come there. As he lectured me I
began to wonder at the little tenderness I had felt for him.
He now looked so self-satisfied, his face the wide, fleshy
face of a frog. With his frog's tongue he wet his lips. He
made no allusion to the last time we had seen each other,

as though our physical awareness of the other had shifted back to its original, blank state. But I remembered him, his wide shoulders, his soft belly. Then he said, "Well?"

"What is my husband researching? Is it dangerous?"

"Dangerous? In what way?"

"Something has happened. I don't know quite what, he won't tell me. Is he in some kind of trouble?"

"No, no. There is nothing dangerous about his research. Dangerous maybe for his career, nothing else. He believes that he's found a fundamental error in the basic precepts of mathematics that disproves everything that came after it. He believes he is on the cusp of developing a new system of numbers that will change the way we understand the world."

"What is it?"

"What is what?"

"The error?"

"Two and two is not four."

"Two and two is not four? What is it, then?"

"For that, you'll have to ask him."

"Why didn't you tell me?"

"To be honest, I didn't quite know the extent of it until a few days ago. The maths chair and I had a long chat."

"Two and two is not four. Could it be true?"

He answered me with a look.

"Will you help him? My husband?"

"How can I help him?"

"I don't know—there must be some way—"

"I'm a professor, not an ayah. I can't force him to study this and not study that, to do this but not to do that."

I was pleading. "He needs help."

"Go home to your husband. He needs a good wife to pack him lunches. That's how you help him. You be good and gentle and kind to him and make him feel like a man." He fixed me in his gaze. A brilliant man, but not a good man, I knew that now, too late.

Then I was back outside, in the widening morning. The sunlight was sharp and dripped into my eyes. They were having a parade, the city of Mainz, another parade, for there had been two or three already this month. The parades, my husband told me, would stop only in March, after Lenten time. The thought of him waking embarrassed or frightened clenched around me. I didn't want him to wake alone. But though it was not very far to the flat, the streets were dense, nearly impenetrable with people. There was a marching band, loud brass, and the music was meant to be cheerful, but it hit my chest with a booming menace. I remembered the firecrackers that went off in the streets at home during parades, a wild scattering of noise that was so unlike the orderly racket of the marching band— it had never occurred to me that it would be a noise I'd miss. In the heart of this noise I thought: My life is starting. For a moment I felt a frenzy that was like happiness. Then the marching band moved farther down the street and the clamor lessened. In its place was a hideous group of Punch-and-Judy puppets, larger, even, than human-size, with enormous red noses and fat cheeks. But there were no strings—people, I realized, in painted masks. The masks were large and heavy looking, three or four times the size of the true heads underneath, but the bodies bore them lightly as they ambled down the street, clowning for the children who sat on the shoulders of their parents and clapped their hands and laughed with delight, pointing their chubby fingers. I tried to let my terrified heart calm, thinking, people not puppets. The expressions on the masks were contorted with delight, delight that came like an agony upon them, and I could not calm. I could not calm and I could not hide my face. I could not pass until the procession was finished. I could not stand still. But what choice did I have? I stood and watched as the puppets made their way down the street. I stood there until the procession was finished and the street was cleared, and then I walked home to my husband.

THE LAUGHTER ARTIST

DRUNK. SPLIT ALMOST open. And I found myself laughing at the window at the violence outside, a man yelling at a woman who walked quickly away from him, crossing through the dark, sudden emptiness of the street to its opposing sidewalk. The violence was his word to her, *cunt*, which is his word to me too, though I was, of course, an unencountered stranger: it was just that the word implicated me. Called out as he moved toward the fleeing woman, trying to master the distance between them, moving toward her like he would take her by the throat. No knife, no gun, but he had his weapons: his arms, his dick, his voice. Call the cops? I might. The phone in my hand. But I didn't know what the cops would do for her, I couldn't be sure they wouldn't make her life worse. And I should—should I—rush down there with a broom and scare him off her, scare him away from her? Yes, of course, that would be the good human thing. The thing to do when you live here though, is to stand at the window and watch with the phone in your hand. Across the way you can see the neighbors in the window doing the same thing. We stand all in our windows like a hall of gods watching, and I am the only one who appears mirthful, I am the only one to laugh.

A laugh signifies. Not just mirth. I am a laughter artist. Artist is certainly a little overblown, though it is actually also my official title. Artist, if I deserve it at all, because I don't just have a single good laugh, but many of them. I have a harsh laugh, a hissing laugh, a soft laugh, a mocking laugh, a laugh that is pure joy, a sweet bell rung, an angry laugh, an instigating laugh, an infecting laugh, a polite laugh, a comforting laugh. I am developing a laugh that incorporates tones of barking with a dog's whine: It is a begging laugh. A laugh that says please. Can one say please with a laugh?

Yes. Listen:
hak-ha-rauh-hak-whoop-oop-ha-hak

Him: Do you want it? Tell me, do you want it? Cunt?
Me: *hak-ha-rauh-hak-whoop-oop-ha-hak*

That was not what I laughed when I saw the man chase the woman across the street. The empty street because the light before it was red, otherwise it was quite busy, cars drove fast there and on rainy days their tires made a sound on the pavement that was oddly comforting, and the tires got sheened black by the water. No, it was not raining, not that day. But it was dusk, and it had been dusk all day. The woman wore a red sweatshirt with the hood pulled up over her head, but I still read her as a woman. I'm not sure why but most women have a walk, they can't help it. Not a swagger hip-walk, or not that it's anything delicate. It's perhaps just an awareness of how much space they are taking up at all times. Even if they take big steps to move quickly they are aware of the precise amount of space their body uses as it expands and contracts. She had that. I had it. I had seen a video of myself moving. It was a play I was in when I was trying to be an actress and not a laughter artist. It was not that I didn't want to be a laughter artist, I just didn't know that you could. In the play I was a waiter and I entered the stage in a manner that I thought was masculine. I was also concentrating on not dropping my tray which was large and circular and which I had to hold at ear level as the director had instructed. On the tray was a soda in a glass bottle of the time period for realism, so if I dropped the tray it would, realistically, spill fizzy across the stage. I can't blame my lack of masculinity on my concentration though, because in fact I practiced for many months, even though it was a small part—a very small part, if I'm being honest, just one scene. I used to go and sit at the bus stop and watch the way people walked, really study them. I made all my friends walk circles around my apartment holding a large circular tray at ear-level, and my husband. I mean, I made my husband do it too, and I filmed them. I watched the films over and over again.

This is when I noticed the thing about women and the way they walk. Walking is not so simple as putting one foot in front of the other, I also learned. Our balance looked both practiced and precarious the longer I studied. I felt sorry for each and every one of us bipeds by the end of it. In contrast, the cat's movements never held the kind of danger that every step for every person seemed to hold. She also never seemed sad.

The cast went out for drinks after the show closed and I was talking to the director. I told him all this. I was a little tipsy and I was apologizing to him for not being able to master a truly masculine walk. But when I apologized he looked amused. He said, "I cast you for that very walk." His words were slurred and tinged with French. "Why do you think I made you a man when you could have been a woman? I liked to see a woman crossing the stage, wishing she were a man." Also, he told me, "You have a careless way of being in your body. It is odd for an actress. Actresses are always very conscious of their bodies. But you, you seem to be shrugging into it. Saying, oh well." I didn't like that very much, though I got the feeling he had meant it as a compliment. I think he had said it almost flirtatiously. But he was married to the lead actress, the one I served a soda to, so maybe it wasn't meant to be a compliment. And the woman rounded the corner.

And the woman rounded the corner, and was erased. The man too rounded the corner and was erased. The street filled up with cars, released by the red light into the pen of the dark block like bulls. Their taillights were red, and their headlights wet the street, darkened it. I tapped the glass like an aquarium, still laughing, but this was an honest laugh, my true laugh, which I only was able to release when I drank, because I was becoming too practiced. Whenever I started to laugh in company I felt like I was constructing the sound, I was choosing between sounds, to give my listener pleasure or deny him it. The choice was mine but I was still making a choice. After a while, even when I was by myself I became too conscious of the choice and the construction to laugh truly. I left my laugh is what I am saying. I stood outside of it and watched it leave me, slipping or bursting through my lips. It was like an ice-cream seller who still liked ice cream but she could not exactly taste it. Or she was too aware of it. She tasted cream, fat, sugar, the light and dark notes of vanilla. It was just too much. But drunk: ah. My laugh returned. The mind forgot the lips, the breath. It fell out of me. It was not a laugh I could perform on command, like all my other laughs. It was a fantastically ugly sound, grating, like a rusty gate swinging open in its hinges:

hareek-hareek-hareek

It felt so good along my throat and rushing past my teeth. I stood at the window for several more minutes. Then my drink was empty and I went to the kitchen to refill it. I live alone in my apartment now and my husband is not my husband. We split amicably and we still see each other sometimes and give each other hugs. I have started whispering something indecipherable into his neck during these hugs, because I am trying to reverse the slow but total erosion of mystery that occurred in the six years of our marriage. The shape of a body, the body's intimate noises, lovemaking, laughter, the muffled farts from the bathroom, the body's weeping; and there were times I had been with him when I was no different than I was as a child, and I suspected that he was no different with me than he was as a child, stupidly happy, and playing, wrestling on the bed like naked kids. The screen dropped from my self in those moments without me even realizing it; the terror came later, when I noticed it had fallen, when I was trying to gather myself up in raw handfuls, but I was like sand all over. I couldn't explain it to him, or even to myself, this absurd panic. It took hold of me when I cooked dinner, or tried to read a book, or sometimes, immediately after we fucked: and he could tell, if he was looking, he described it as going blank behind the eyes. Still cooking, still moving my eyes across the page, still lying beside him, loose and breathing—the body lived and lived. But panic expanded outward, irrepressibly outward. What was I afraid of? Nothing. Literally nothing. Nothingness. Of vanishing.

For my final project in laughter school, I created a divorcée laugh. It took me some time to articulate and then perfect. I started with the pure laugh of a baby and then made it dirty, roughed up the edges. I had to perform it in front of my class and my professor, and as they watched it burst from my mouth I felt myself becoming the person the laugh suggested, broken but swaggering, the kind of woman who leaves lipstick marks on a cigarette. Afterward my professor took me aside and asked me if I would teach it to her, which I was happy to do, sitting almost knee to knee with her in her little camphor-smelling office. She learned it after only a couple minutes and capped the laugh off with her own, bitter flourish: then it was hers, though she was happily married to an accountant. She herself was a beautiful, seamless laugher, her face seemed to pull back a layer as it laughed so you could see its elegant structure, its bones. She taught laughter as though it were a foreign language, demonstrating a laugh and then breaking it down to its plainest syllables, which she would feed us two or three at a time until we could laugh it in unison, then we would break out into our own rhythm, and the laugh would shatter across the room. It sounded different in each of our voices: Lawrence's Malbec baritone, Jessa's creamy mezzo-soprano, Lilly's surprising tenor; Timo thrust it all through the nose, but in Sandra you could watch the laugh rise up from her gut to her chest to her shoulders, it was deeply athletic, and she told me she had to wear a sports bra to class because it created as much breast-joggling as running. I could pick my classmates out in a room of laughers now, and when I hear their voices on TV or in commercials I remember quite viscerally the body that created the musical sounds: it is intimate as touch, their laughter. We're not in touch now, but sometimes we will call each other and laugh into the receiver,

laugh and listen, as we learned how to do. The laughter
school I went to is the best one in the country though it is
not a degree-granting program, all you get is a certificate.
I have mine hung up in my living room, and I am proud
of it. I am proud of it, but I was terrified to explain to my
Indian mother what I had spent my time and money doing.

But when I actually told my mom that I was a laughter
artist she said, "Professional laugher? Like a professional
mourner?"

I had never heard of that.

"When your uncle died, we hired professional mourners, these were ladies who would come and weep and wail.
They'd walk in the funeral procession with us and they
would weep and wail."

"But why?"

"Sometimes, when you lose—when people die—it is
very hard to make tears. You feel like you want to make
tears but something inside you stops them and they press
your chest. Like something sitting on it. So these ladies
come and they cry for you. When you hear them cry your
body starts to make tears, the tears travel up from your
chest and into your eyes. And when they flow from your
eyes that weight on your chest decreases."

I wanted to touch my mother. On that funereal day I
had been separated from her by a continent and I didn't
understand why she had left. My parents tried to explain
death to me, but I didn't get it; I never saw my uncle who
lived in India, his goneness already seemed to me a fixed

state; now double gone, he was an abstraction beyond com-
prehension. But years later I saw a picture of her she had
taken for my father, who stayed behind, with me. In the
picture she was wearing a white sari and the skin around
her eyes was very dark, her hair shorn close to the scalp,
bald as a newborn, lips parted—her smile was breaking.
She looked dense and fragile and beautiful as a star.

I told her that there were practical applications like
voiceover work and studio audience work, and that there
was the laughter I developed on my own, like an artist who
made drawings for advertisings but was also a painter in
the 1940s. I wanted to emphasize the practicality of my
new profession because I could hear fear in her voice when
she told me about the mourners. I was a wild girl, she was
afraid for me. I couldn't stroke away her fear.

I learned fear from her, my mother.

The street cleared and emptied many more times, and
the moon came out. By that time I was finished laughing.
I went and took a hot shower that was somewhat brief
though it was my third one of the day. It was becoming
difficult for me because we were in a terrible drought, but
bathing gave me a relief that was intense and medicinal.
Three degrees more and the water would have burned my
skin, it was on the knife's edge of tolerable, and I used dish
soap, in fact I pretended I was a dish, and handled myself
very gently. I had been bathing this way for the last three
days and my skin had become very—tight. It seemed not
to fit me so exactly anymore, like it used to, as though I

was wearing a perfect glove that had been designed for my hand. Now it felt like the inside of me was growing faster than the outside of me, and soon I would split myself open. The girl inside would be clean and shining, golden. One had to be careful when one was drunk and bathing, one might slip and shatter oneself. But truly she would not be golden, I knew, when she emerged. She would have the horrible pink skin that was left when the sunburn peeled away: newborn, ugly and defenseless like a little baby mole.

I was dressing when the phone rang for awhile and then I jumped at the sound of the buzzer and went to the window and looked down: my ex-husband was standing in his jacket looking up and waving at me. We were too far away to see the expression on each other's faces. I let him up. He seemed to want to touch me, but he was holding himself back from it, I had a bristle all over me, I was so tense. I hadn't slept for two days and it was nearly the night of the third. He said my name, which is Janaki, which I will never fucking shorten to Jan. You don't say the *Jan* in Janaki like the *Jan* in Jan: you stretch it out and soften it. I taught it to my class and my professor like my professor taught us laughter, breaking it down to its velvet syllables. It was my grandmother's.

"Hi Ravi." It came out almost like a yelp. My throat was rough from all that laughing.

"You okay, buddy?"

"What are you doing here?"

I looked at him, his body. I had formed against him, my

shape had shaped to fit him. Now, separate, we seemed so odd. He wore his worry all over him, but there was nothing he could do to soothe himself like he used to.

"Janaki?"

I was falling asleep on my feet, something I had not thought possible. My eyes jerked open. Vertigo. I put an arm out and the wall held me up. What on earth? his face was saying. I still had that bristle on me so he didn't try to reach. Me. If only I had learned earlier to quill myself. A crumple between the brows. Such a handsome divorcé.

"You drunk?"

"Yup. So?"

"So nothing. Just wanted to make sure you weren't having, like, a stroke."

I smiled. "No droop."

"Okay, why don't we sit down."

"Okay. Don't patronize me."

"I didn't think I was."

"Tone."

I sat down on the floor. He might be surprised how neat the apartment was, now that I lived alone. When we lived together I assumed an anti-housework position that sprang from our collective confusion about what a wife was. Even my own shit, my clothes, would pile up around the dresser and the bed in formations he called berms. Now, I often put the clothes I discarded in the hamper, or right back on the hanger. "Want some. Whiskey?"

"No thanks." He sat down too, awkwardly. His legs

didn't fold easily into cross but frogged up at his sides. My stupid husband. He loved a woman named Sophie now, and I intuited that Sophie would be pregnant soon; she was a little older than us and wanted kids, and I know this because she told me at dinner the very first time we met. He had said in the car that it was his fault, which was vain and infuriating besides being untrue. Your fault? As if he had any kind of control over my life, let alone the things that happened to me. If we hadn't gotten divorced, you wouldn't have gone on that date. We both wanted the divorce. In fact, the divorce was my idea. My idea, my fault? And then he was backpedaling, saying no one's fault, no one's fault. Which is incidentally what the state of California had said about our divorce and would say about my rape. No one's fault. Not enough evidence. Your word against his.

"Let's get you to bed."

"If you had the chance to go to the moon, would you?"

"Yes," he said.

"What about Mars? Mars you don't come home."

I could feel him looking at me. "Look at you, you can hardly keep your eyes open."

"Moon yes, Mars yes. For me. Actually moon yes Mars maybe."

"Jaan."

"You don't get to do this anymore."

"Jesus, someone has to. Up."

I was lifting myself to my feet. His hands were cold and familiar. For a moment I remembered my body. Then it became too heavy. I was in bed. The old days were over, I understood, the awkward easy days of living freely. What lay ahead felt austere and frightening. In fact, I couldn't look at them full in the face. I shut my eyes.

My professor told me that she had accepted me into the program because my laughter was unique and troubling and she saw potential. But I would have to learn how to blend. That was an odd comment to me because I thought of myself as perpetually blending, a child-of-immigrants instinct that I was working very hard to unlearn, because it made me a bad actress. But my instincts had always been different with laughter: my laughter professor told me to blend, but she also said she had a laugh she thought would be perfect for me. I went to her office with the hope that I would be her protégé, a hope I didn't bother to disguise, I was so eager to mentored. In fact, she did become a mentor to me and to all of us, all of us who wanted to be mentored, and she didn't play favorites. She gave us each a laugh to learn that was ours.

Aroof—aroof—ek—ek-ek-ek

It took a while. "More guttural. Spit it. It has blood."

I didn't understand yet that some laughs are not happy. It was a powerful dark noise she made, an incantatory sound, barely controlled, controllable. The laugh changed her face, her kind, maternal face, made it snarling. The bones stood out. We spent a long time, several hours, on those tiny syllables, and she was more patient than I was: I was hungry. Then I laughed a long thread of it, accurately if not expertly, it fell out of me like a strand of red silk, and in the stillness of that room, I sat flushed with my own daring, my own blood.

"What's it called?"

"You already know the name of it."

There was a tiny moon in the window of her office, tiny because it was alone in the window and there was nothing to compare it to but itself. Fall. "Death-laugh."

"Ah. What kind?"

"There's more than one?"

"Of course," she said.

"Laugh-in-the-face-of," I said.

She was not smiling. "Yes."

DIDI

WHEN I GOT back from the grocery store, my wife was sitting in an armchair and looking out the window at the rain. She seemed startled to see me, and wiped away her tears with her palms, and then I could see her carefully arranging her face before she turned it to me.

"Back so soon?"

"The bus came right away."

"Did you get everything?"

"Yes, everything," I said. I went to the kitchen and put all the bags of groceries down on the counter. I liked the strain in my arms and my shoulders and was sorry to let the bags go. They slumped down. My wife padded in behind me and went to the sink to wash her hands. She was wearing a beautiful dress of a dark, fine material that she wore sometimes when we went out on rare occasions to fancy restaurants. Now that I got close to her I could see the makeup on her eyelids and smell her perfume. It was eleven thirty in the morning.

"Where are you going?"

"Where would I be going?" she said. She lifted each item out of the grocery bag carefully, turning each orange over in her slim hands to inspect them or bless them. She took out a large wooden bowl and placed the oranges inside, and she was right to do so; they were beautiful in that bowl.

"Those are cara cara," I told her. "I had a sample in the store."

"How much were they?"

"Four-fifty a pound."

"*Four-fifty!*" She looked displeased, and I was honestly glad. I wanted to see something on her face, even displeasure.

"Try one," I said.

"I'm not hungry right now."

"Here," I said. I took one out of the bowl and peeled it messily; the juice got all over my hands. My clothes were still damp from the rain outside. I held out a section to her. "Here, try it."

She stood with her arms folded. She took it up like a game: angry wife, foolish husband.

"Here," I said. The fruit was a reddish orange inside, almost the color of a grapefruit. I came toward her, holding the piece in my hand. She stood still. I brought the fruit to her lips. "Here," I said, putting the fruit right to her mouth, wetting her lips with the juice. She looked very small, standing with me in the kitchen. Her dark hair was parted neatly at one side and gathered at her neck. She had wide-set eyes and very narrow shoulders. She didn't resist me. Her lips opened. She ate the piece of fruit I offered her, and then opened her mouth for another. So I stood there and fed her the orange. I was grateful to her. When we were finished she wiped her mouth.

In the bus earlier there had been enough room for me to sit down and put the bags of groceries on the seat beside me. I was in a sort of trance when I looked out the window. It was the sound of the wheels on the rainy street and the rain splattering down on the window. I hardly knew where I was. I had an urge to lift a bag of flour from the bag of groceries. I took out the bag of whole-grain flour and sat it down on my lap. I wanted to feel the weight and heft of it in my arms. I put my arms around it and closed my eyes. For a little time it felt right, pressing down into my thighs, bouncing with the movement of the bus, almost like a live thing. But after a while I began to feel unsatisfied and I put it away.

"Why are you dressed like that?" I said now.

"Oh," she said absently. She was looking out the window again. "I just wanted to feel pretty."

During this time my wife made bread every day, too much bread for just us, so we would walk around on Saturday mornings and give the loaves away to the people who lived on the street in our neighborhood, though we often got the feeling they would have preferred something else. We thought about getting a dog. My wife occupied herself during free time by teaching herself Hindi. I had my books; sometimes I went alone to bars. We spent some quiet months. I saw her eyes track the children in restaurants or in the park. Once on the way out of a pizza shop a little boy grasped her hands with his little fingers and tried to climb up her leg, saying, "Mommy, Mommy!" It was when he saw her face that he realized his mistake and skittered off, and when I put a hand on my wife's shoulder, she turned away from me. Again, I could see her carefully arranging herself. When she looked up I saw she was trying to laugh.

I had taken to telling the story, when my wife was elsewhere, to strangers at parties. After a few beers I would have a nice feeling in my stomach. It was a warm anger. I would say, "The worst part, I mean the really fucked part is that I'm not even sure I want to be a father. In fact, I think that it is fundamentally evil to bring life into this world. You think about the things you know your child must suffer, any child, even if you give him the best life you can. Think about death, for example," I'd say. "Think about the carrying capacity of the earth, for god's sake," I'd say. "Think about pedophiles." We stopped getting invited to so many parties.

There was a way my wife touched her stomach a day or two before she told me. I saw her gathering her strength. I gathered mine too. The nine months were like a single held breath.

Then our daughter was born. When she was a baby I liked to listen to a particular song by Echo and the Bunnymen on the weekend and watch her kick her legs up into the air. By the time she was five I knew she would never be pretty; she had all of my looks. She was stout, solidly built, dark as me or darker, with thick brows and small, curious eyes that peered out of her face like a badger's. Her name was Diviya: we called her Didi.

"You ever think," I said to Didi, "that you and me just sitting here at the table is going to only be relevant to us?"

"No," said Didi. It was a Sunday morning and she was smacking down a glass of milk; she was a big eater, and ate always with relish.

"I mean, when I die, and when you die, this moment is not going to matter to anyone. Nobody else is here."

"Mom's here."

"Mom's in the other room."

"It'll matter to me."

"Well, you'll be dead."

"No, I won't." Then she took out her *101 Vacation Jokes* book and read some jokes aloud. She had learned to read early, and at six she was working through *Wuthering Heights*. I was afraid that her idea of the world of adults was getting skewed, but supposed she'd sort it out eventually. She was sitting at the kitchen table and swinging her legs off the seat while I drank my coffee. "Why do I love omelets so much?"

"You don't like omelets."

"No, the joke person likes them."

"Okay, why."

"Because they're egg-cellent." She had a deadpan delivery.

"That's so bad it physically hurts. Anyway, what does that have to do with vacation?"

"Beats me," she said. She read, "Disney and I have something in common. We both love a happy ending."

"A *what*?" I said.

"A happy ending. I don't get it."

"No," I said. "Oh no. No, no, no. Let me have that book." It was written by some asshole named Nicholas Trevor. I showed it to my wife. She was in the bedroom, reading a book of Hindi poems. "We have to burn this book," I said.

"I think you may be overreacting."

"Do you even know what a happy ending is?"

"Yes," she said. "I know what a happy ending is."

I sat down on the bed with her. Something about the way we were positioned, her lying on her back with her book and me very close to her, not touching her, reminded me of when she was pregnant with Didi, and I had put my hand on her belly for the first time and felt a live thing kick. My wife told me her senses had sharpened. "It's so strange," she had said. "I can smell everything. I imagine this is what the world is like for a dog. Even though the window's closed I can smell the rain on the street, and the wet grass and dirt." She told me I smelled like eight different things and listed them all, the last one being nervousness.

"What does nervousness smell like?" I asked her.

"Sort of a sour smell. It's in your sweat."

"You can't smell that."

"You're not nervous?" she said. She grasped my elbow with her hand. I was almost angry with her for noticing. "I'm nervous too," she said. But pregnancy had given her the calm radiance of a Buddha, and I didn't believe her.

"What are we going to tell Didi?" I asked her now.

"Tell her about what?" said my wife.

"Sex, death, happy endings," I said.

"Oh, I don't know," she said. "Everything, I suppose."

In high school I was a wrestler. I remember being quite good, though at some point I just gave it up. I can remember very vividly that smell of sweat and the deodorant and the powder we wore under our shorts to keep from chafing. Closer down to the mat there was the odor of feet, the sticky plastic of the mat too, and I loved that smell because I didn't allow myself to smell it unless I had won.

There is one particular match I think of often. It was one of the last matches I had, before I gave up wrestling. Before a match I would try and make my mind cool and blank. I needed to feel no emotion toward my opponent. I thought of myself as a soldier in some ways. I listened to the voice of my coach—he understood me. He knew it was not the things he said to me but the sound of his voice, and he used his voice to talk to me the way one uses their voice to talk to a child or an animal, with attention to pitch and tone.

My opponent and I were in the same weight division,

but he had an immense presence, the presence of a bull, and he was dark-skinned like me, his ancestry similarly tropical. At first I avoided eye contact with him, because I was struggling to clear that space in my mind. Each time he met my eyes I felt as though I had brushed against a thin, prickly thing, like the spine of a fish. But I didn't want to seem weak or frightened, so after a while I began to meet his eyes. I fixed his face in my mind—the same flat contour of South Indian nostril, the purple-brown lips—his head was shaved like mine, and like me his ears stuck out almost sweetly, and when his mouth opened I could see his teeth, slightly tinged with yellow, irregularly shaped, nearly shining against his dark skin. Close enough that I could see the pores in his face, and I began to make all sorts of novice mistakes, giving him too much ground when I should have been on the offensive, staying up high, though my true strength is in my legs. All of a sudden he caught me in his arms. He stood behind me, hugging the breath out of my stomach and chest. At first I felt pure panic, and then another emotion came through. The emotion was almost a sound I heard, ringing in my ears. I lay back into my opponent's arms.

I woke up to the sound of the phone ringing. Didi was at a sleepover; it was too late in the night for good news. I raced to the phone.

"Hello?"

"Dad?"

"Didi?"

"Hi, Dad." She was whispering.

"What's the matter? What's wrong? Are you okay?"

My eyes were beginning to adjust. I took the phone with me back to the bedroom, where the light from the street poured in from the windows, and sat down on the bed. "Didi," I said to my wife, who rubbed her eyes with her hands, looking for a moment like a child. I took her warm foot in my hand.

"Will you come get me?"

"Didi, what happened?"

"Is my bed still there?"

"Of course your bed is still here. Did something happen?" But I couldn't get an answer out of her. I had almost never heard her frightened before. It was her first sleepover. I covered the mouth of the phone with my hand and explained the situation to my wife, who said that we would go get her in the morning. "I told you she was too little for a sleepover," she couldn't help adding. It had stopped raining, and I began to put on my pants and shoes. "Honey, it's two in the morning," she said, and then, sighing, "Take a taxi, at least."

But I walked. It was warmer outside than I expected. The sky was the kind of bruisy purple that it was in early mornings before rain, almost red, an eerie glow. After I crossed Valencia the streets were empty. As a young man I had walked like this, before dawn in the city streets, when I couldn't sleep. People told me it was dangerous, but I saw all sorts of things. I liked to stand at the corner and watch the traffic lights change even though there were no cars. I was the last man on earth, but the lights would still change. I would wait my turn.

Didi was sitting on the top step outside her friend's apartment with her backpack on. She was wearing yellow pants and a pink sweatshirt she had outgrown but still insisted on wearing.

"What the heck are you doing, guddu?" I said. It was strange to see her there. She tilted her face toward me so the light washed down over it. Nobody will have this picture of her—not her mother or the man who will take her away, for it will die with me. My daughter's brown face in the light from the street, the glitter in her black eyes.

"I didn't want to wake anybody up," she said.

"Come down from there," I said. She climbed down the steps very carefully, holding on to the railing. We began to walk. "Are you tired?"

"No," she said. She held my hand out of habit. Her other arm swung free. She was growing quick; she might reach my waist, it felt, in a matter of weeks.

"What happened?" I said. "Were you scared of something? Did you have a fight?"

"I thought you were going to give my bed away."

"That's absurd, Didi, we would never give your bed away."

"Well, that's what I thought." The two of us waited at the light, even though there was nobody coming. All the neighborhood cats had come out, the shy ones that skittered away if they saw us during the daytime, but at night they were free and hissed if we got too close. "Do you ever feel sad when you go to the library?"

"Do you?"

"Yeah," she said. "I feel like there are just so many books there and I will never be able to read them all."

"A lot of those books aren't even good books. They're like cookbooks and books on computer programming."

"Oh. So you don't feel sad in the library?"

"Sometimes I do."

I had been walking quickly, and she lagged a little behind me, so I slowed. It was a great pleasure to watch her move. She gathered her hands into fists and marched, full of destination. "Why were you worried we were going to give your bed away?"

"Well, there are all these friends who sleep outside. Mom gets really sad to see all those friends outside. So I thought maybe since I wasn't using my bed she would give it to one of them. I don't mind just for the night, but tomorrow I would need my bed again and what would happen if he didn't want to leave? Would we have to share it? Why do those friends have to sleep outside, anyway?"

It was a question she asked frequently, and never seemed satisfied with an answer. So I just shrugged. "I don't know, Didi. Some friends sleep outside, some friends sleep inside. But we would never give your bed away."

"I know *you* wouldn't, but what if Mom wanted to?"

"Mom knows that your bed is your bed, even when you're not using it, okay?"

"Okay," she said. Sometimes I still couldn't read her.

"Didi, there's something I want to tell you. You had an older brother."

"I did?" she said. "Where is he?"

"He died, before he was born."

"What kind of person was he?"

"I don't know," I said. I looked down at her. I could see the thought of a brother moving around in her brain. Still I pushed her. "His brain wasn't fully formed, so he died."

"Died?" said Didi. Then she said, "Like all those people in Japan."

"Kind of like that," I said. We crossed Valencia Street, a strange press of people because the bars were all closing, and they seemed shocked to see Didi, standing so small and fearless among them. Drunk people have their own logic, I suppose. I lifted her up. It was that old myth, Krishna's father carrying baby Krishna on his shoulders, the waters rising to touch the child's feet. I held on to her shins, her feet knocking against my chest; she wrapped her arms around my neck and leaned forward so her chest was against my head. Then we crossed Valencia and the streets were empty.

"Dad, what happened to those people in Japan?"

"They died, Didi."

"I *know*, I mean, what happened to them?"

"They drowned," I said. "Or something fell on them. Or maybe some people had heart attacks."

"But what *happened*?"

She was on the edge of it. I held on to her. My shoulders began to ache.

"I don't know," I said. "What happened?"

"I don't know," she said.

The hill up to our house was steep. "Didi, can I put you down?" I said.

"Okay," she said.

I knelt so she could get down. I thought of her brother. For a moment I could see him so clearly, standing beside her on the sidewalk. He had the face of that high-school wrestler I surrendered to, which is to say, my own face. His arms hung down at his sides. It was with a terrific anger and love he had wrestled me all those years ago. Didi trundled along beside me. Then we were home. I lifted her and took her to bed. I took off her shoes and her socks and put on her nightie that was still in her backpack with her toothbrush and her joke book and her copy of *Wuthering Heights*. I sat in the dark with her in her tiny room until she fell asleep, which was not very long. The night air had kept me awake; now here in the warm house I felt old and sleepy. I felt sleep begin to hold me, as I imagine death would, gently around the waist. For a moment, I was sorry. Then I lay back into it.

A HOUSE IS A BODY

NOT THE SCENT of the smoke, but the sight of it, not the sight itself, but the screen through which it altered the sunlight—she couldn't articulate the change exactly, it's just that the light seemed odd, like the sour light of a nightmare. She had overslept. She was used to waking at the sound of his alarm. Risen dazed and blinking into this odd day, the cool and yellow morning. Before she woke the girl, she stood on the deck. I have use of my limbs, she thought, without knowing why she thought it. And went back into the house. She dressed the child, and combed her hair, and shook cereal into a bowl for her—the child seemed not to notice anything at all, still pliant with sleep, and ate without speaking but with an unfocused concentration she brought to most tasks, that she brought even to her dreams, her face concentrated even in the task of its dreaming, mirroring perhaps a dream-face that rarely smiled. It was too late now to hurry. And the girl ate slowly. The mother had the urge to smack her. She turned her eyes down to her mug of coffee and took a sip from it. Without milk or sugar it tasted only of acid. Drank. She was coming awake.

Where's Daddy today? Halfway through the soggy bowl.

Went to work early. You know, he might get home late tonight. After you're in bed.

I feel funny, said the girl.

Funny how.

Shrugged.

The mother put a testing hand against the silky forehead. You're fine.

I feel funny.

No, she wasn't fine, the forehead was hot. But jesus, god, just a moment alone, today of all days. Children made noise, the woman had been told, but nobody had ever told her that the noise children made would be intolerable. The noise they made, the sneezing and singing and screaming and shrieking—nothing wrong, when she raced to the other room, the child was shrieking with delight—and crying, crying, a scraped knee, a broken doll, and the crashing of toys and furniture and bodies, this noise was near constant, slowly growing throughout the waking hours, swelling in the afternoon to an evening crescendo, the noise under everything, diminishing every pure thought and action, the noise she could not quite block out but had to monitor for signs of true distress. Even alone, one child—christ, imagine two! looking down at the sick daughter. She was small, she was six years old, very small, but turning, already, or she should say finally human, with her own thoughts. Dark as her father, darker than him, the mother had not made a mark on her.

Okay. Stay home with me today. I'll call the school. You go back to bed.

I don't want to.

You go to school or you go back to bed.

No.

Don't try me right now. The anger in her own voice scared her. The girl fled. Anika!

She called the school. Something going around. She was shaking. The anger in her voice sounded like her mother's.

Anika?

She lay in her bed, still with her school clothes on, and pressed her face into the pillow. Now the mother was gentle, and stroked her back. The structure of her rib cage was like hands, ribs had an affinity with slender fingers. The little body contained a soul. She wasn't crying, but her face was flushed.

Come let's get you—

No!

Let's get you—Anika!—*still*—

For she was squirming, then shivering, as the woman lifted the dress over her head, and pulled down the tights. Her baby's body gone skinny, the ribs, the dark chest, tiny nipples. Her pajamas were pink, they buttoned. She dressed the girl in them, then tucked the blankets around her.

Still cold?

She nodded.

You'll warm up.

Read to me?

The same book, one they could both easily recite by memory (father too). The mother made herself patient. *One winter morning, Peter woke up and looked out the window.* The body beside her felt incandescent. She could have been sick the day before and the mother hadn't noticed. Maybe even two days. Had she? Three pages and she was dozing. The mother shut the curtains and left the room. Out the window the sky was lambent: glowing, it seemed, from a diffuse source, and she went on the deck to gaze at it. The air felt dry in her throat. The hill sloped away from the house, bare for a mile and then trees, not tall enough to block the view yet, but they were creeping slowly upward, and one day would. The woman was remembering the hillside when it was green, and jeweled with newts bisected with purple and orange, with sideways eyes, cool on the palm, their movements slow with terror. The girl had caught them. Delighted. They lost their tails, she told her mother. If they were caught. Does it hurt? The mother didn't know. What happens to the tail, does it become a whole new newt? The mother said maybe. And then the girl's eyes lighting up with understanding: *is that how humans are made too?* Baby, the mother had asked, do we have tails? But rain had not come for months and months, and the hillside had browned—some would say become golden but she would say brown, and it was not bitterness, because she had felt this way for many years, steady in her hatred of summer.

The light was golden. As light should be but never is. Then she caught the first dark scent. Oh—*what now?* But the feeling was like wonder. Smoke? She was a body in air. As he was speaking, last night, she could hear the water in his mouth—his spit—she could hear the sounds of the mouth that happened around the words, of the lips opening and closing, of the tongue sliding, and occasionally the click of teeth. Under the sound of the words was the sound of breath, the breath that carried those words, so at first it was difficult to hear them, the words, and when she did hear them there was so much space around them she thought, "Well, I'm okay." But later, only a little later, she realized that it had been shock. She had not let the words into her body. It was as though she had placed a pill on her tongue, could feel the weight of it there but could not yet taste it. Alone, in the almost empty house— for it was late at night, and the girl was sleeping—his words began to enter her: she tasted them, she felt the burning of their swallow, she felt them come into her bloodstream. She stood in front of the mirror. He had changed her, she wanted to see it. Her features were the same, but they had a different meaning now, she looked older, and sour, and she saw the lines on either side of her mouth, and traced them with her finger. The lines of her mother, her mother's sourness. Oh god. And then she turned away from the mirror with a clenching, a balling up, for once her tears began to form she would not be able to stop them, for days she would live in a dazy red and swollen mind, stuffed up as if by cold, and eyes always leaking in betrayal.

Inside she turned on the TV for news, but there was nothing. Only soaps. Three channels came in, and a Spanish channel, and a Christian one. Switched it off. And restless. She went into the child's room. Sick, the girl was docile, hers, she was her mother's but not her own, too docile, suffering, but the face in sleep was angelic. She had forgotten to take her temperature like a bad mother, she had not given her any medicine like a bad mother. Should she wake her? But didn't the body need sleep most of all? She had thought of the drive to school with her daughter, pulling to the curb, and watching her walk into the stone building. Past that, she had not thought, but likely she would have ended up at the ocean. Walking, walking, or just sitting in the car, dry, watching the sea fold over. Where was he. Work, or.

Startled by a knock at the door, she looked through the window in the kitchen and saw a man standing in uniform. He started speaking as soon as she opened the door, polite but with little preamble: the hillside was burning. Far off but uncontained, growing in the other direction: still. Are you all right?

She nodded. She was not sure what shape her face had been in to make him ask.

It's not going to come this close. I promise you.

Then why do we have to leave? She heard herself

speaking like a child. The man had a face, she noticed, a young face, dark with stubble, the kind of man who couldn't keep his chin clean. The eyes of the man were amber with pity under his hat.

Just a precaution. Really. There's no need to be afraid.

Do we have enough water?

What?

To put the fire out.

Helicopters, he said, come from the lake.

Is there enough water in the lake?

No need to worry. We're just being extra careful.

Don't cry now, she told herself. Then it won't stop. She watched his Jeep turn in the drive and she waved to him.

She stood looking dumbly at the possessions they had gathered and arranged. Each thing was in its place with few subtractions; he had taken only a few shirts and pants and a beloved sweater she sometimes borrowed and two books (he didn't read often, and they were just paperbacks, easily replaceable). Each thing was in its place and clean because she had just cleaned. She liked to scrub the kitchen floor on her hands and knees: he liked it too. She went to the kitchen and opened the utensils drawer and looked down at the spoons. Which should she take? Would they melt? She began to take them out of the drawer and put them in a paper bag with handles. And then the forks. Not the real knives with teeth but the gentle butter knives, made for spreading. Then she took out the utensil holder and put that in the bag too. Undressed, the drawer looked unsettling. She took off her wedding ring and put it in the drawer and closed it, hard, she could hear the gold ping against the wood.

Mommy.

In the doorway of her room as if in the frame of a picture: but who would paint a child like this, skinny and wary—the eyes of it oddly yellow. Her baby.

Go back to bed, Ani.

I was sick in the bed.

What?

I was sick.

She had spit up, like a baby, her breakfast, sour in the sheets, and on her nightclothes. The mother undressed her and pulled the foul clothes off the bed. Heat came off the body of the child as it would a radiator. Now the mother would be a good mother, lifting the girl, who smelled sweet in her hair, and taking her to the bathroom, and running a bath, as she waited, wrapped in a towel on the toilet to keep warm. The mother poured a spoon of blue medicine down the girl's throat, bitter, but she told the girl of Shiva's heroism, sucking the poison from the ocean as it was churned by the gods for nectar, and holding it in his dark throat so the rest would not be harmed. Will I turn blue?

No, love. Why so tender? And tears suddenly rising. In you go.

Have I been bad?

No.

Then why are you crying?

You're just sick. Sometimes when people are sick they throw up. It's okay.

She washed her daughter's hair. The girl was having trouble keeping upright and wanted to lie down. Her head bubbled under the water for a few seconds as it followed its own weight. Almost, said the mother, patting her body dry. She brought a too-big T-shirt for the girl and slipped her arms and neck through it. Forcing her tears back into her eyes took all her effort. But she wiped her face and turned to the girl and smiled. Okay, Ani, back to bed.

In her parents' bed the child looked tiny.

The man looked disappointed when she opened the door. The open door let in the friendly smell of smoke, the kind that perfumed the hair of campers.

I fell asleep! she said.

The thing is, the fire's turned. We're evacuating everyone now.

Is the lake dry?

He rubbed his chin. They're dumping mud.

I have to pack.

There's not much time now.

No time to pack?

Ten minutes, he said, okay?

Fifteen?

No, ten. Five. But I can't come back here to make sure

you're out, you should be out already. Will you be out in
ten minutes?

Like a child she was making him a solemn promise.
Could he see that underneath her skull was glinting with
laughter? But she straightened herself: she was a serious
woman. She set an egg-timer. His car raised dust as it
turned.

A house is a body, a body houses souls. Three souls but
now there were only two. The house did not betray pain.
She would just as well let the photographs burn, but the
girl would want them one day. What would the girl want?
It was time, past time, to call him, but still she did not. She
filled a paper bag with books and when she lifted it by the
handles it tore in half. Once I had been beautiful. Not all
at once but for a day at a time. And now—

Outside the yellow of the air had intensified, the light
had thickened from golden to something more. There was
no time, but she stepped onto the deck anyway, and held
her arm out, it had changed color. Her skin looked eerie,
ruined. She could not see the fire from where she stood,
but the smell in the air had deepened, that good smell, the
clean smell of wood releasing its carbon. And the aircraft
hauling water from the lake thrusting their noise into the
morning. They were small as insects.

Anika?

She was sleeping with her mouth open, she couldn't
pull open her eyes, she was sweating her kid's sweat at her
brow, the gentle kind of sweat that smelled like clay. The

bad mother had forgotten to take her daughter's temperature, but to take it now she would have to wake her, and she couldn't remember if she should; it had been at least a year since the girl was so sick, maybe longer, her colds were mild and almost sweet, cured, it seemed, by a day of rest, hot tea, baby aspirin, and a mother or father sitting on the bed and singing, badly (mother) or beautifully (father). She didn't trust the internet, but Dr. Spock would know, she went to the shelf and remembered she'd emptied it into the bag, she rifled through the spilt bag and found him, flipped to the index, fever, fever, and then to the page it directed. It was a good sign if your child was sleeping, if she was able to sleep then the fever wasn't so severe and you must not wake her. Still, it was alarming to put her hand against the cheek or the forehead of the little girl— surely she had never been this hot. At the child's neck the skin prickled up in the shape of a continent, raised and slightly purple. She winced when it was touched by the mother's gentle fingers and the skin under the fingers: even hotter. Spock? Now don't get hysterical. He only took one suitcase so she could still pack, none of these paper ripping bags. And then they'd drive straight down to the hospital and she'd call him from there. The egg-timer sounded, she cranked it again, generously granting herself more time as though she had the power to grant it.

What should she take from the house, just the pictures? And the clothes from the girl's room she lifted from their hangers and set them down on the bed. Perhaps—food?

The air coming from the girl's lungs had an odd flavor. Spock gave you the feeling that everything was under control, he had written a whole book on all the possibilities, they were all accounted for. Her jewelry wouldn't burn, but perhaps it would melt, the bridal jewelry she had been saving for the girl: a crust of jewels for the neck and the arms and a complex and delicate gold structure worn in the hair and the ear lobes and nose, even if neither were pierced. And the bride wrapped in silk and strung with gold and jewels looking shy up into the eyes of the new husband, whom she has loved, and already fucked, but still shy, enacting her ritual part, and he too shy, enacting his ritual part, though they laughed as the priest made him promise that he had regarded her only in friendship before this moment, and they had each thought of a secret corner of the other: a dark nipple held between teeth, a dark cock gripped in a pale hand. Under the turban, three gray hairs at the crown of his head, she knew, and the fleck of subtle color in the iris of his left eye. And he to her: the curves of her, the location of several moles. The jewelry was stored in a crawl space above the kitchen, which required a ladder, and she climbed it, and hoisted the box which contained it down, nearly losing balance and toppling over, and where would she be, but finding her footing and giddy as her feet touched the kitchen tile. But this was the wrong box, full of letters, tinder, difficult to look at. She could see his hand. He stroked ink onto the page neatly, his writing was angular and precise, an architect's hand, while her long scribble imbued several possible meanings into each word; he squinted over them, the months she spent in Kenya doing fieldwork and they had not been able to email because she was too remote. And had talked only once, his voice rushing toward her from another continent, she had wept afterward, missing him. That missing him had felt like pain, but it was sweetness, she knew now, that came with certainty. She climbed up again. At the top of the ladder she saw black ash on the skylight. The light had changed again. Pulled out the box but the child was crying.

Ma!

She climbed down. A flock of helicopters growling overhead. She pulled the girl up. You could read a book by the light of that body, limp in her arms, smelling faintly like eggs.

Ma, I saw a blobby thing! With teeth—and—She was out of breath.

There's no blobby thing. You were dreaming. I'm going to take your temperature, okay?

I wasn't dreaming. I had my eyes open just like now.

There's no blobby thing. She raced to the bathroom, and came back with the thermometer. Open.

The child's tongue had a fur of white. The egg-timer was sounding again. Hold on.

She twisted the thing quiet. The thermometer read 104 degrees. The girl lay back in the enormous bed. Jesus, kid.

Mama, look, the blobby thing is there. The mother

winced at "mama," the word the child had outgrown, now creeping back into her mouth.

Okay, she said, talking to herself, I'm going to take the photographs, and take the jewelry, and we're going to go. We're going.

Go where?

To the doctor.

The girl began to whimper. Mama, I hate the doctor. Mama, I hate her she gives me shots. Mama, please don't make me go.

Don't call me that. She hated that word. It made her think of a sweater with stains on it. Mama. A cow with huge teats. The girl was gearing up for a tantrum, but instead the energy seemed to be leeching from her, her body softened and she shut her eyes. What does death smell like? But don't panic, she was saying to herself. Too late to panic. The rash on the neck of the child looked alien, unlike the rest of the child, which, even hot, felt silky and familiar. An animal knows her young. Could she lick the fever away, or suck from her neck the poison to hold in her own throat. She was not thinking clearly.

Anika, we're going now, but the girl's half-shut eyes only showed the white. Ani?

Through the window, her eye caught the edge of it: the fire. Then, picking up the girl, she was back out on the deck, entranced. Look, Ani, but the girl would not look. The light of the day blackened and remade new. Waves of black air were blowing toward the house, streaming up from beyond the trees as though the ocean itself were burning. She felt their bodies acutely in air, in air that had the harsh, milky quality of evening. Lit. She was nearly gasping. Look, Ani, she said again, lifting her daughter's head. Look how beautiful.

NIGHT GARDEN

I HEARD THE BARKING at six thirty or seven. It had been a long, hot day, and evening was a relief. I was cooking dinner. I knew Neela's voice well, the bright happy barking that he threw out in greeting, the little yips of pleading for a treat or a good rubdown, and the rare growl, sitting low and distrustful in his throat when the milkman came around—he was a friendly dog. This sound was unlike any of those. It was high, and held in it a mineral note of panic. I went over to the kitchen window that looked out onto the yard, where we had a garden. There was a pomegranate tree, an orange tree, and some thick, flowering plants, jasmine and jacaranda, and some I did not know, that my husband had planted years before. But I was the one that kept them alive. Neela stood dead center, in the red earth. His tail was taut and his head was level with his spine, ears pinned against his skull, so his body was pulled into a straight line, nearly gleaming with a quality of attention. He was not a large dog, reddish and sweet and fox-like, sometimes shy, with dark paws and snout. Facing him was a black snake—a cobra—with the head raised, the hood fanned out.

I myself let out a cry. The cobra had lifted the front of her body at least two feet from the ground. I had never seen one so close, even separated by four strong walls and a pane of glass. I could see, even, her delicate tongue, darting between her black lips. Her eyes were fixed on the dog, and his on hers. Their gaze did not waver. Her body too was taut with attention, shiny back gleaming from the low evening light. The sky, I saw now, was red, low and red, and the sun a wavering orange circle in the sky.

Of course my first instinct was to rush out screaming and scare the thing off. But something stopped me. I stood for a full minute at the sink, shaking all over. Then I took a deep breath and phoned my sister.

"There's a cobra outside with Neela."

She exhaled. She was my big sister, and had been subject, lately, to too many of my emergencies. "It's okay. Call Dr. Ramanathan. He knows about snakes. Do you have his phone number?"

I did.

"Are you crying?"

"No."

"It's okay, Viji."

"I can't—" Then I stopped myself.

"Can't what?" My sister has a voice she could soften or harden depending on circumstance. She kept it soft with me now, like talking to a child. I wiped my face, like a child, with the bottom of my shirt.

"I'll call back," I said.

I went again to the window. The animals were still there, exactly where they had been when I last looked. The dog had stopped barking, and the cobra looked like a line of poured oil. I dialed Dr. Ramanathan's number.

"Doctor, there's a snake out there with my dog. A cobra. In my yard."

"A cobra is it?" I could see him in his office, his white hair and furred ears. He had a doctor's gruffness, casual in the most serious of circumstances, and had seen both my children through countless fevers, stomach upsets, and broken bones. "Has it bitten?"

"No, they haven't touched each other. They're not even moving. Just staring each other down."

"Don't do anything. Just watch them. Stay inside."

"Nothing? He'll die," I said. "I know it, he'll die."

"If you stay inside the house, he won't die. The snake was trying to come inside the house, and he stopped it. Now he is giving all his attention to the snake. If you break that concentration the snake will kill him, and it will also be very dangerous for you."

"Are you sure?"

"No one must come in until the snake has left. Tell your husband to stay out until the snake is gone."

After I hung up with Dr. Ramanathan, I took a chair and set it by the window, so I could sit while I watched the dog and the snake. It was a strange dance, stranger still because of its soundlessness. The snake would advance, the dog would retreat a few steps. The hair was standing up on the back of his neck, like a cat, and now the tail pointed straight up. I could see fear in his face, with his eyes narrowed and his teeth bared. The snake looked in comparison almost peaceful. I didn't hear her hiss. The white symbol glowed on her back. Their focus was so completely on the other. I wondered if they were communicating in some way I couldn't hear or understand. Then the dog stood his ground and the snake stopped advancing. She seemed to rise up even higher. There was something too perfect about her movements, which were curving and graceful. Half in love with both, I thought, and it chilled me. Evening came down heavily, the massive red sky darkened into purple.

The phone rang. It was my sister.

"Well?"

"They're still there. They've hardly moved."

"Viji have you eaten? It's getting late."

I had been in the middle of making a simple dinner for myself, and had of course forgotten. The rice was sitting half-washed in a bowl next to the sink, the onion was chopped and raw. I didn't feel hungry, less, even, than usual—I don't like to eat by myself. Instead, I felt hollow, like a clay pot waiting for water. It was pleasant, almost an ache.

"What time is it?"

"Nine-thirty, darling—eat something. Shall I come over?"

"No! Dr. Ramanathan says no one can come in or out."

"You phoned Susheel?"

"What's the point?"

"What if he comes home?"

"He's not coming."

"It's his dog too."

"My dog," I said, too loudly. "He's my dog."

Then back to the window. It had grown dark. I hesitated to turn on the light in the house, in case they would startle. Our eyes all sharpened as the light faded. There was a bit of light that came in from the street, from the other houses, though it was filtered through the leaves and branches of the fruit trees and the flowers. In it, I could see the eyes of my dog, bright as live coal. There is a depth that dogs' eyes have, which snakes' eyes lack. Snakes' eyes are flat and uncompromising, and reveal none of the animating intelligence. Maybe I could learn something from that. I sometimes think there is too much doggishness in me.

Now, very quietly, I could hear the snake hissing. There was a rough edge to it. The dog advanced. The snake seemed to snap her jaws. I have seen a dead snake, split open on the side of the road. Its blood was red and the meat looked like meat, swarmed with flies. People said it was a bad omen for me, a bride, to see it then. Imagine the wedding of the Orissa bride, who married the cobra that lived near the anthill, and was blessed by the village.

People made jokes about the wedding night, but everyone's marriage is unknowable from the outside. I saw a picture of her in the newspaper, black hair, startled eyes, and I blessed her too—who wouldn't? This same communion, it must have been, two sets of eyes inextricably locked, for hours. The kumkum smeared in her part like blood. The dog was gaining ground. He stood proud and erect, still focused but doggish now, full of a child's righteousness. His ears pricked up. But then, for no reason I could discern, the weather between them turned, and it was the snake who held them both, immense and swaying, in her infinite power.

Who knows how much time passed. I sat there by the window. The three of us were in a kind of trance. Once, I awoke with my head in my arms, I had fallen asleep right there on the lip of the sink. I blinked once, trying to make sense of the kitchen's dark shapes. It seemed as though I had had a dream of a snake and Neela, engaged in a bloodless, endless battle, and when I looked outside there they were, keeping this long vigil. Their bodies were outlined by moonlight. At this hour, they looked unearthly, gods who had taken the form of animals for cosmic war. But I could see the fatigue in my dog. You see it with people on their feet for hours, even when they try and hide it, a slump in the shoulders, the loose shoulders of the dead. No different with my dog. He would die, I was sure of it. I pressed this thought against me. The empty house. I would let all the plants go brown in the yard. I would move.

I find that at night, you can look at your life from a great distance, as though you are a child sitting up in a tree, listening to the meaningless chatter of adults. I stood up in the kitchen. It had been years since I was up this late. Slowly, infinitely slow, the creatures were inching back, toward the shed at the side of the house, the dog retreating, the snake advancing. Their movements were like those of huge clouds that seem to sit still in the sky, and you mark their progression only against the landscape. I followed them, moving from one window to the other. I became very angry with Neela. What arrogance or stupidity had urged him to take on this task? It's easier to be the hero, to leave and let others suffer the consequences. To run barking into the house was all he needed to do, to show me the snake so I could close up our doors.

I stood. The snake hissed up, and made a ducking move forward, toward Neela, who snarled, baring his yellow teeth, doing a delicate maneuver with his paws, shuffled back, weaving like a boxer. He let out three high yelps, pure anger, and snapped his jaws, and the snake rose even higher, flaring out her hood, hissing, I could hear it, loudly, like a spray of water. Then she lowered herself. Back and forth on the ground as she slunk away, leaving her belly's imprint on the dirt.

I went outside. The air was clean and cool, thin, as it hadn't been all day, almost like it had rained. He was tired. He whimpered when he saw me, his ears pricking up, and pressed his wet snout in my hand as I got close. He was radiant. With his mouth pressed closed between my hands, his eyes looked all over my face, joyful and humble, the way dogs are, filled with gladness. He swayed on his feet with fatigue, then slumped down to his knees in a dead faint, tongue lolling back. His breathing came out slow and easy.

Who had death come for, the dog or me? I lifted the sleeping creature in my arms. He was no heavier than each of my children when they were young, and I took them in my arms to bed. The air was very still outside at this time of night—or morning. Hardly any sound came from the street, and all the lights were off in the neighboring houses. The air rushed in and out of Neela's body, his lungs and snout. What you have left is what you have. I carried him into the house.

ACKNOWLEDGMENTS

MY DEEPEST THANKS:

To the extraordinary Samantha Shea. To Betsy Gleick and the wonderful team at Algonquin. To the institutions that have supported my work: Vassar College, San Francisco State, the Millay Colony for the Arts, Hedgebrook, Blue Mountain Center, the San José State Center for Steinbeck Studies, the Elizabeth George Foundation, the San Francisco Arts Commission, and Kundiman. To the Ruby and Rachel Khong. To the San Francisco Public Library and its Friends.

To Laura Furman.

To my teachers: Josh Harmon, Maxine Chernoff, Kiese Laymon, Candice Lowe Swift, and Peter Orner. Traci and Jay from the California State Summer School for the Arts. Melissa Sanders-Self.

To dear readers and friends: Meng Jin, Rebekah Pickard, Marco Lean, Adam Gardener, Chris Freimuth, Catherine Epstein.

To my family, especially: Asha Pandya, Sanjay Iyer, Merylee Smith Bingham, Ed Bingham, Josh Bingham, Hansa Bhaskar, Beena Sharma, and BY Swamy.

To Shamala Gallagher.

Most of all, to Abe and Kavita. The joy of you both astonishes me.